CHARLIE'S PRIDE

CHARLIE'S PRIDE

a novel

Dee Hubbard

To Nancy—
As long as I'm in the room, you'll
never be the oldest one there!
Thanks for a lovely evening,

Dee Hubbard

2015
FITHIAN PRESS
MCKINLEYVILLE, CALIFORNIA

The interior design and the cover design of this book are intended for and limited to the
publisher's first print edition of the book and related marketing display purposes. All
other use of those designs without the publisher's permission is prohibited.

Published by Fithian Press
A division of Daniel and Daniel, Publishers, Inc.
Post Office Box 2790
McKinleyville, CA 95519
www.danielpublishing.com

Cover painting by Eldridge Hardie

Distributed by SCB Distributors (800) 729-6423

LIBRARY OF CONGRESS CATALOGING-IN-PUBLICATION DATA
Hubbard, Dee, (date)
Charlie's pride : a novel / by Dee Hubbard.
pages cm
ISBN 978-1-56474-568-2 (pbk. : alk. paper)
1. Racially mixed people—Fiction. 2. Indians of North America—Fiction.
3. Children—Death—Fiction. 4. Marijuana—Growth—Fiction.
5. Klamath River Valley (Or. and Calif.)—Fiction. I. Title.

PS3608.U2323C48 2015
813'.6—dc23
2014025755

*For the men and women who stand
behind the flyfishers, our fishing guides;*

for Bonnie, who also knows where the river sings;

*and for all my children,
Mark, Laurie, Jenny, Jill, and Dale,
who taught me when to listen*

ACKNOWLEDGMENTS

I AM GRATEFUL to the Denver Public Library for invaluable help with research in the writing of this novel. I read everything I could find in the library about the ethnology of the Klamath Indian tribes—their beliefs, their values, and their economy. In researching the marijuana plantations in the national forests of Northern California over the past twenty-five years, as well as the details of gold dredging on the Klamath river, I relied on feature news stories and magazine articles. Information concerning the geology, orogeny, flora, and fauna of the Klamath comes mostly from David Rain Wallace's natural history classic, *The Klamath Knot.*

The native language and mythology in this novel are mostly products of the author's imagination, and are intended to honor spiritual unions of our Native Americans with their natural world.

CONTENTS

CHARLIE'S PRIDE

TO CHARLEY

PROLOGUE

HE RUNS FOR THE JOY of running—fast and free. Without a planned course or destination and without a conscious seeking, he relishes pleasure in the moment. Caution is a concept as yet unlearned. Obstacles are minor irritations to overcome. He challenges even the wind.

Deceptively strong, the boy's slender legs propel him through a sea of purple and blue wildflowers where old blends with new. Hillsides feed an alluvial meadow, and ebbing life nourishes fresh life, as larkspur, fading in decline, flows into mountain gentian, robust in first bloom. Ever-changing blossoms measure the passing of seasons. During nature's annual cycle of renewal, the meadow celebrates symmetrical beauty in its repetitions of birth, life, and death. Through the meadow he races, and his unbroken track weaves a channel toward the unknown—his future, his destiny.

Capricious breezes drive azure ripples, undulating like ocean swells, across the flowers behind him, playfully chasing him. When they catch him, his restraining headband fails, and his long, black hair reverses direction and sweeps in front of his eyes. He swats at wind-driven snarls blurring his vision. Then, realizing air currents can be his ally as they are for his namesake, he raises both arms and rotates them so his hands can capture the wind. With palms at a forty-five-degree angle, he sprints in long arcing turns, first left, then right, moving his arms up and down to imitate wings flapping in flight. Pursing his lips, he emits a series of piercing high-pitched whistles—the hunting cry of a Northern Goshawk, king of the accipiters. Absorbed in his simulation, he stumbles on an unseen rock and almost falls. Laughing at misfortune averted, he regains his balance and makes throat sounds mimicking a rending crash. Then he slows to a walk and screams, "Ay-e-e-e," and repeats, louder, *"AY-E-E-E."* Echoless, his imitations of a raptor's call race away to join a departing breeze.

A small stream winds through the meadow, etching its surface into a pattern of curling loops like interlocking pieces of a giant jigsaw puzzle. He stops at the inside of a loop, and his eyes search along its sandy bank. *Whoever passes leaves his sign here, Papa said.* Kneeling down, he examines three sets of fresh tracks, two small and one larger. All show similar pads with no points, indicating retracted claws. *Bobcat, a mother with two kittens. Papa showed me tracks like this last week.*

A departing trail of damaged flowers beckons, and the boy follows it up a sunny knoll. Disturbed soil in a bed of pink phlox reveals where the kittens began to play. For a moment, he closes his eyes and imagines them batting at each other with their paws, snarling and mewing with sibling rivalry and mock hostility. Then he reaches down and plucks several soft brown tufts of fur that mark the location and fierceness of their combat. Similar signs farther on show him where the kittens wrestled back down the hillside, turning over and over in patches of asters and wild geraniums. He sees where their mother rushed in to restore peace in her family.

His pursuit concedes to midsummer lethargy, and he lies down, spread-eagled in a grove of wildflowers. Wind-woven blossoms of pink and white petals dance above him in the sky, like clouds of fluttering butterflies. When he closes his eyes, he hears a busy buzz of feasting bees and the crisp, flutelike whistling of a now softening breeze. Exhaling through his mouth, he forces his chest and belly to constrict until he's satisfied all the stale air is gone. Then he inhales.

Fragrances from a thousand sources rush in and swell his lungs near to bursting.

TAWAHANA
Where the River Begins

*W*ITH A MOTHER'S INSTINCTIVE concern, she watches him from an open kitchen window. He approaches
through the back yard, first skipping, then slowing and scuffing
along, head bowed as if lost in thought. *He's growing so fast,* she
thinks. *Outgrows jeans before I can patch them and doesn't need
to roll up his shirt cuffs anymore. But his shoes. Look at them. Not
outgrown, just abused. Must he always take the most difficult path?
And must he always be home so late from school?* She shakes her
head in despair.

His school books are tethered to his father's old deerskin
belt. He slings them on the back porch, places his lunch pail beside them, and takes a few steps away. Then he hesitates, frowns,
kicks at the earth in front of him as if it were a barrier, and returns to sit on the middle step. *Restless, always restless,* his mother
diagnoses. Removing his headband, he shakes his hair, releasing
it to the wind, and leans back, his elbows on the top step. Then
he closes his eyes, smiles, and tilts his head at a slight angle, as if
listening to something far away. Relieved to see her son relax, his
mother starts to call out to him and then places a hand over her
mouth, stifling the impulse. *When he's like this, he hears and sees
things the rest of us don't. He's alone in a world I can't enter.* She
sighs and turns away from the window.

OCTOBER'S afternoon sun feels good on his cheek. Autumn
rains are late, Indian Creek is low, and he has to strain to hear its

friendly *K-chug...K-chug, K-chug...K-chug* as it gurgles around its last meander a hundred feet away. No strain for him to hear the rest of its course as the creek dips under Highway 96 and loses its friendliness in a furious cataract that rushes into the Klamath gorge and down to the river below. The familiar sounds produce their usual effect, and the boy's imagination drifts his mind into a magical world that lures him further upstream, where the river begins. Its beckoning is invisible and silent, but irresistible, like the pot of gold at rainbow's end his mother sometimes talks about. He isn't sure what his imagined world contains. He thinks elegant unicorns and friendly dinosaurs might live there, maybe some gentle, playful Omahs whom his father once described as giant children of the Gods, and maybe even trout so big a boy could harness them and ride the river, like riding horses bareback in the fields.

When he opens his eyes, his images disappear. He looks up to a forested V in the hills where Indian Creek enters the valley, his approved boundary limit. He rises and takes a few steps toward the creek. Again he hesitates, then sighs, shakes his head, turns and retraces his steps. Not enough time for another exploration before dinner. He'll do his homework now. He also forms a different resolve.

HIS face reflects unboyish seriousness as he waits patiently for his parents to finish eating. When they're done he gazes first at his father, then at his mother, and asks, "Papa, Mama, I want to follow Indian Creek higher, beyond the upper meadow in our valley."

Parent reactions are sourced in different genders and different ancient cultures: his father's, pure Hupok Indian; his mother's, a Celtic mixture of Scottish and Irish.

His father nods his head up and down in silent approval, a barely perceptible movement of his neck muscles with no accompanying display of emotion. *It's time,* he thinks. *My son needs to develop self-reliance and a strong body, and he should pursue his own understanding of his natural heritage.*

His mother shakes her head from side to side in silent but vigorous protest. "No, not yet," she whispers to herself. Her eyes flash fear. *I can't let him go wild. Not yet, not at eight. He has so much wisdom for his age, shows too much promise for a better future than he can find here…among river dwellers who remain locked in yesterday. My son needs to challenge his mind, not his body, and stay connected to his heritage of literature and education.*

His parents' unspoken but different responses aren't lost on the boy. Hoping he hasn't started an argument, he drops his gaze but not his request.

Reticent by nature and reluctant to speak first, his father waits, his face impassive.

"Why, Tamiko, why, my Little Hawk?" his mother asks. As he lifts his gaze to hers, she sees earnestness in his eyes. Then she hears it in his voice.

"It's so hard for me to stop and turn back at the end of our valley," he says. "It's like…like I have to see what's around the next bend, what's above the next meadow."

"Can you tell me why you're so restless?"

"I don't know why, Mama." He struggles to give better words to his thoughts and finishes, shaking his head, "It's a strong feeling I have but don't understand."

"I…I think I understand," she says, trying to suppress the tremor in her voice and another instinctive headshake. *But, must I accept the inevitable so soon?*

His natural stoicism, part of his father's legacy, is overcome by stronger emotions, and Tamiko pleads with his mother, first with longing in his eyes. "Please, Mama. If I'm always where I can see or hear Indian Creek, I can't get lost."

"No, Tamiko, the fear I have is not that you'll get lost, at least not on Indian Creek." She turns to face her husband. "He must keep up with his studies, complete his education. No truancies, like other Indian boys. In my classroom, their chairs are too often empty."

"I also dream of a better life for him," his father says, understanding and accepting her concern. He looks across the rough wooden table to his son. "Can you do both, Tamiko? Can you follow that part of you which comes from me and draws you toward the river and its wild places, and also follow that part of you which comes from your mother and draws you toward the world of learning and accomplishment?"

The boy thinks for a moment. When he answers, he looks first at his mother and then at his father. "I don't know, Papa. I think I can. And I'd like to try. I feel both of you pulling inside me, but it doesn't feel like you pull me in different directions."

"Such a mature answer," his mother says proudly. Rising from the table she wipes tears from her eyes and then stands behind her son, her arms encircling his shoulders. "Soon you will be too embarrassed for me to do this," she whispers in his ear. She ruffles his hair with her fingers—a mother's caress—kisses his cheek, and then laughs with natural gaiety. "Go find your pot of gold, my untamed young son. But always remember you are child not just of a wild river and an ancient culture some still call uncivilized, but also of a modern civilized society that blends many cultures."

"I will, Mama." He returns his mother's embrace and kiss, his small arms stretching to encircle her neck. "Thank you, Mama. I'll remember."

A hint of a smile forms on his father's lips. "Tomorrow my son, I will draw a map for you. We'll study it together, and then you'll make a copy. My copy I'll put behind the kitchen door. Whenever you go off exploring, you'll write down the date and show your destination and the route you plan to follow. Your copy you'll carry with you."

"Yes, Papa, I will."

"Now, I have something I put aside for you in the year of your birth." Tamiko's father excuses himself. Soon he returns and places a long white feather, black barred and black tipped, in front of his son. "I've saved it for a time such as this. It's from the one whose Indian name you bear, the great hawk of the north, largest and most fierce of our Klamath hawks. Wear this in your headband as a symbol of your freedom to wander without boundary and travel beyond a parent's watchful eye. It will help keep you ever vigilant, ever safe."

Tamiko's eyes shine. "Thank you, Papa," he says as he runs to his room to find his headband.

THAT evening, wearing his headband with its new embellishment, Tamiko approaches his father where he sits beside the season's first fire, smoking a pipe. The boy sits cross-legged on the bare floor at his father's side, presses his arms on the armrest, hands touching his father's arm, and asks, "Papa, have you been to where the river begins?"

"Yes, once. Many years ago. Before you were born."

"What's it like, Papa?"

His father's expression grows dreamy. "Yes...where the river begins...Tawahana, our people called it. You have unusual and special feelings for the river, and it's time you knew about its origin. The river is first named at a great waterfall where it escapes from Klamath Lake. Many years ago the government located a vast reservation there of one million acres...for the Hupoks and all the Klamath tribes. But our people are foolish. Foolish and lazy. Many of them forget how to work, and now they sell their lands—to get money to buy things they once considered unnecessary. Soon only a small part of the reservation will remain. But this is not Tawahana. The river actually has two beginnings, both above Klamath Lake."

The father pauses to refill and relight his pipe. Tendrils of blue smoke curl above his head. Tamiko is impatient for his father to continue, but remains silent. Unnoticed by both, his mother enters the room. She stands silently in shadow, listening and watching firelight silhouette the scene before her on a rough paneled wall beyond. The feather in her son's headband sends an elongated shadow above the fire-lit circumference, like a spire extending into the heavens.

The father resumes at a slow, deliberate pace, his rarely used storyteller's voice. "The ancients called one beginning Wadunga, the river's fury, and the other Wateela, the river's peace." The father notices his son's questioning expression. "Names you haven't heard?" he asks.

"No, Papa. You've not spoken them before."

"I thought not. Those names are no longer used, almost forgotten. No one thinks to keep the old names from our history in spoken use."

"Wadunga...Wateela," Tamiko repeats. "I won't forget."

"No, you won't forget. I'll describe both origins in the way I was first told. You must remember, and you must tell your sons, and they their sons, in just the same way."

"I promise, Papa."

The father resumes his narrative. "High above the clouds that surround the wet mountains of the setting sun is a deep blue lake, the deepest lake in all America. It fills the inside of a topless mountain. This mountain is a volcano that blew apart many centuries ago and is no longer active. When the mountain top exploded into the sky, it became a dark cloud that covered the sun for a year. The remaining crater is an angry place, a very strange and mysterious place where winds blow that never cease. Nowhere does water flow into the lake, and most believe it is the mouth of a giant river flowing up from a freshwater ocean far below. Raging fires burn near the center of the earth and heat the ocean until it boils, but the river cools as it weaves its way up and into the lake. Although the water loses its heat, it was once cursed by the Gods, and it retains dark powers that can burn the souls of men forever."

Hearing a stifled "O-h-h-h," the father pauses to look at his son, smiles, pats him on the head, and then continues. "Fish cannot long survive in the lake, and it's barren, except for small trout men plant there each year. Its shoreline is unbroken, and nowhere does water flow out of the lake; however, the volcano is badly faulted with many cracks and fissures. So the lake leaks from hundreds of hidden underwater openings, and its water escapes down the mountainside.

"Hupoks shun the mountain because we believe it's a battleground of the Gods, where during the night you can hear the wind scream curses of Gods wounded in battle. We believe all water flowing from the mountain carries this rage from the Gods. This beginning is Wadunga, the river's fury."

The father's gaze leaves his son's face, and he stares into the fire, as if drawing memory from its flames. Tamiko shivers and frowns. Wadunga sounds ominous, not the place for unicorns and dinosaurs to play, or for small boys to harness and ride big fish.

After a moment's silence, the father continues. "Far away in high desert plains of the rising sun, parched earth captures water from occasional rains. Many tiny seeps and rivulets form and flow deep underground so the sun cannot steal their water to moisten his sky. Finally, when they have joined and are strong enough to confront the sun, they emerge from the ground as sapphire blue springs, deep in a pine tree forest different from any you've ever seen. It's a calm and quiet place guarded by minks, wise owls, and all-seeing nighthawks. These springs never freeze in winter and are so clear you can see down to a depth of ten men. Their water once was blessed by the Gods and is so pure that it possesses magical healing powers. In the springs swim large trout the color of fire and ice, whose flesh contains mystical compounds that produce strength and wisdom." The father pauses to glance at his son, sees Tamiko is smiling, and then continues. "These trout are the only pure descendants of what your mother calls our primordial fish, the first trout who spawned all steelhead who roamed the Klamath before the coming of man. Many streams flow from these springs and join in a huge marsh where no man can walk. There, cheerful voices from a thousand different birds and animals fill the air with song. Blossoms of ten thousand different flowers, plants, and trees scent the air with perfume.

"Hupoks revere the forest and marsh because we believe these are gardens of the Gods, where during the day you can hear gentle breezes whisper laughter of Gods at play. We believe water flowing from the gardens carries blessings from the Gods. This beginning is Wateela, the river's peace."

Tamiko claps his hands. Wateela is more like he's imagined. "Are there unicorns and dinosaurs in the gardens, Papa? And Omahs?" he asks, his voice now animated.

His father chuckles. "No, I'm afraid not. Perhaps once. Long ago. But none are left now."

The boy's disappointment is visible. "And the trout, Papa? The big trout? Are they so big I could ride them bareback, like a horse?"

"I'm sorry, my son." The father's voice is gentle. "The trout are very big but not so big a boy could ride."

Then Tamiko brightens again. "Not even in the middle of the marsh where men can't go? In my heart, when I close my eyes and listen to Indian Creek, I sometimes see big trout there, or someplace like it."

"No. Not even there. Not even in the middle of the marsh."

"But, how do you know, Papa? If no one has ever seen the middle of the marsh?"

His father's brow furrows, and he thinks a moment. "Perhaps you are right, my son. I can only tell you the wisdom of men. And what do they know that they haven't seen? What is seen in a young boy's heart may be a greater truth. How can I tell you what man doesn't see doesn't exist? I cannot. How can I tell you what you see only in your heart does exist? I cannot. For I too am only a man who sometimes sees too much with his eyes and too little with his heart. Always respect what you see in your heart. Believe it. And someday it may be so."

The boy's curiosity lingers. "Tell me more about the two beginnings, Papa. Where does their water go?"

"Although they are as different as day and night, for they rise in dawn and dusk, these two beginnings are both very beautiful. They finally join far beneath the surface of Klamath Lake, so the river we see here is blended equally with fury and with peace. Our Klamath River remains true to its origins, for it alternately rages in fury and glides in peace all the way to the sea where the sun finally sets."

Tamiko's eyes are rapt and shining. "If I keep following Indian Creek, will I find Tawahana some day Papa? Will I find the battlegrounds and the gardens of the Gods?"

"No, my son. Indian Creek is only a small Klamath tributary. Tawahana isn't part of our mountains. It's far north, in Oregon."

The boy puts his small hands on his father's big work-scarred hands. "Will you take me there Papa? To where the river begins?"

"Yes, Little Hawk." The father clasps his son's hands and presses gently to seal his promise. "Someday, I will take you there. I will show you both beginnings." He pauses and looks deeply into the boy's eyes. "Yes, Tamiko, my Little Hawk, with your gaze so piercing. You may indeed see at Wateela what you now see only in your heart."

DEEPLY moved by the father-and-son exchange, Tamiko's mother withdraws as silently as she entered. Happiness and sadness both assail her. Conflicting emotions threaten to overcome her, and she wipes fresh tears from her eyes. *I've heard a part of his history my quiet husband never talks about. It's a view of how things came to be that has no parallel in my culture.*

That night she slips into her son's room. Moonlight bathes his face, serene and childlike in repose. She smiles when she sees his headband and feather still in place. Removing them gently, she bends and kisses him along the crease left in his forehead. She stands a moment in the moonlight and gazes out the window. *So, have I lost my son to the world of his father's ancestors? An over-romanticized world which time has passed by and can bring my Little Hawk only disappointment and disillusionment? Perhaps not. I will have to see.*

―――――

AT CHRISTMAS, A Schwinn bicycle appears in a corner behind the family Christmas tree, the result of economies by both parents. It's an older model without gears, but freshly painted and newly oiled. Tamiko waits impatiently for winter to end so he can expand his explorations. Then he follows logging roads farther and farther upstream. When road and stream diverge, he hides his bike and walks streamside. Beyond each bend a cloistered, new river mystery unfolds and charms his senses. He watches raccoons feed fastidiously on fresh-water clams, opening shells with their long, delicate fingers and sucking out the meat inside like toothless old Indians. He watches dipper birds dive without fear into raging cataracts and invade the trout's domain, searching for underwater bugs. Bands of exotic color flash before him when startled wood ducks fly from their nests crying their distressed "whoo-eek." When he disturbs their slumber, unseen spotted owls hoot at him. Color plates in a dog-eared bird book he carries stuffed under the waist of his jeans help him identify spring songbirds—the tanagers, the grosbeaks, and the vireos. He listens carefully to their songs, until he can identify them all by sound. Their voices draw him deeper into the mountains.

"Know our Klamath flowers too," his mother urges. So each Saturday he returns home with dozens of new blossoms for her to identify. "Enough, Tamiko," she finally says. "Your curiosity exceeds my knowledge." On rare outings with his father he learns to identify trees and other plants of the Klamath forests.

As he explores higher, he stops to feel shallow gashes left in red firs and hemlocks, where elk rubbed their antlers free of velvet. He shinnies up a scarred old aspen tree to reach higher for deeper cuts, where bears sharpened their claws. His fingers come away all sticky from tree sap oozing from open wounds.

He relishes bold young smells of spring and summer: heavy, intoxicating scents from ravines filled with incense cedar trees steaming dry after a rain; delicate, seductive perfumes from hidden, sun-sheltered terraces graced with the Klamath's wild orchids—pink calypsos blooming after snowmelt, coral roots, oranges, reds, tiny lady slippers—all fresh and sweet, all unthreatened and unsoiled; ripening aromas—often pungent, sometimes even acrid—from tangled, streamside jungles of verdant plants exploding with new growth; mind-drugging fragrances from meadows drenched with azaleas and rhododendrons; and finally, summer's last gift—elusive, wind-driven exhalations from patches of heather newly freed as alpine snowfields retreat from the hot Klamath sun.

More subtle, mature scents of autumn tantalize him: the musky smell of elk in rut, the faint odor of decay from fern groves turning bronze, and the tart, fruity odor—not unpleasant—of fresh scat from bears who feast on wild berries. He learns where the best wild raspberries grow, occasionally beats the bears to their harvest, and stuffs himself until his belly aches.

Sights, sounds, and smells of an immutable Klamath landscape burn deeply into his soul.

THE PALADORA

Pathway to the Sun

TAMIKO TRAVELS ALONE, above buried tracks left by his Hupok ancestors. Bulldozed wider years before, their forgotten trail lies beneath him, under an eroding overlay of crushed rock and gravel. "The ancients called it the Paladora," his father told him, "pathway to the sun. Now it's just another old road with no name going nowhere."

Always too bumpy and dusty or too wet and muddy to bicycle in comfort, the washboard surface once provided access to rich timber stands, now all harvested, above the Klamath River. No visible signs of Indian use remain. "When the white men came, they brought their thirst for gold with them," his father explained, "and then they took everything, even the forests and paths of our forefathers."

Standing to gain leverage for a steep incline, he pulls up with his hands against his handlebar grips and increases his legs' downward pumping power. He breathes deeply and feels his chest swell. His muscles respond with the boundless energy of youth, and his bicycle surges ahead, tires spitting loose gravel.

As the road levels and commands less concentration, something tugs at him from deep inside, a legacy no one can take from him, an instinctive awareness of earlier times. Images of piercing eyes set in dark, deeply seamed faces crowd into his mind, and he feels a sudden warming of his blood, a swell of emotion not related to exertion. It brings a palpable stirring in his breast he's too young to identify, can only feel—pride of heritage. He imagines he hears soft footsteps accompanying the faces, and he wonders if traces of their moccasin prints might endure, preserved deep in the earth beneath him. His eyes bore into the road ahead as if his vision can pierce its surface, remove the present, restore the past, and reconnect it to his future.

The Paladora provided his ancestors with a natural access into the sinuous, seemingly endless ridges and crests of the Klamath's many mountain ranges. Then, a relentless search for wealth by those who came later drove them to follow and improve the same route into an ever beckoning and unknown beyond. When he looks up toward the unknown, he sees rolling hills twist, turn, and writhe like an awakening serpent. Hills become mountains that incline ever upward, then stair-step yet higher and higher until they lose themselves in a bluish haze beyond vision, beyond comprehension. He knows the old road ends just beyond bicycle range. But not beyond his boyish imagination. He's sure the original Paladora resumes somewhere, somewhere toward the sky, toward eternal vastness, and then continues on, deep into the heart and soul of the Klamaths, where even greed must concede to limitlessness.

Someday, he vows. *Someday I will find where the pathway to the sun begins again.*

Breathing heavily, he stops pedaling where the road veers away from the hillside to junction with Indian Creek. There it turns up again, narrows to two rain-washed ruts, switches back and then snakes its way up Superstition Ridge. Mindful not to leave any tracks, he lifts his bicycle off the road and walks it through young dogwood and hawthorn trees growing in the protective shade of an immense Douglas fir, the forest's elder statesman and a solitary old-growth remnant. With its upper branches soaring above its surroundings, the hoary patriarch silently demands his veneration. *How did it escape cutting?* he wonders. Wild rose thorns stab at his shins, and he pauses to roll his right pant leg back down. Concealing his bike in a thicket of more hospitable hazel and barberry shrubs, he carefully avoids tearing any leaves, breaking any stems, or otherwise disturbing the vegetation.

Staccato yammering from jackhammers breaking rock in the basin below him drums into his ears, preempting natural forest voices. He pauses and frowns. He knows the offending noise culprit is a new mine tunneling into the side of a gulch draining the crest of Deadman's Point into Indian Creek's south fork. "Not gold," his father told him. "Jade. Discovered by a young prospector with a college degree. Found a whole ledge of it along that old gold miners' trail. After all the major gold discoveries played out, those miners scratched and sweated in their barren holes in the earth for another forty years. Like blind mice, they burrowed deeper and deeper into the Siskiyou Range, searching for something that wasn't there. They passed that ledge every time they came into town, but they couldn't recognize jadeite. Right there in front of them all that time and they never knew it."

A dozen men now work the jade claim, and he doesn't want them to know of his presence. But he isn't interested in the mine or its riches. He seeks a secluded pool higher up, where two tributaries of Indian Creek join. With over two miles yet to cover on foot and the sun already passing its zenith, he knows he will have to travel quickly or nightfall will overtake him on his long ride out.

From a wire basket in front of his handlebars, he takes a battered lunchbox and removes two chocolate bars, a big red apple, and a thick ham sandwich wrapped in newspaper. The meat he'd scavenged from remnants in a corner of the refrigerator, and the bread his mother had set aside for him from Friday night's baking. Hunger gnaws in his belly, but he resists its ache. Eating now will slow him down.

The chocolate bars slip easily into a partially torn shirt pocket, but the sandwich and apple are too bulky, so he stuffs them under his heavy flannel shirt, next to a torn and sweat-stained map, which he still carries but seldom consults. The newspaper tickles his ribs, but the apple feels cool and refreshing next to his bare belly and gives him goose bumps. He leaves two remaining chocolate bars in his lunchbox—just in case—and carefully conceals it away from his bicycle. He knows if he arrives home late again his mother won't wait Saturday night supper for him, and her blazing green eyes will scold him more effectively than words ever could.

Although he's still hot and sweaty from his long bike ride, he shivers as he feels a breath of cold air envelop him. In March, winter's stubborn chill lingers in surface air along the creek. Removing a bulky wool sweater from the basket, he wraps its sleeves around his waist and knots them in front. He won't need a sweater hiking upstream. Warming rays from the mid-afternoon sun will filter through the trees and sear into him. But he might need a sweater to keep him warm coming back down, when early spring's meager heat suddenly dissipates, the sun races to set behind him, and his shirt, still damp from his uphill sweat, cools rapidly as the temperature dips.

He's taken only a few steps when impulse seizes him. Returning to a rock outcropping that gives him a clear view of the mine several hundred yards below, he watches two miners enter the noisy shaft. Frowning again, he stoops and loosens a fist-sized rock from the outcropping. Rising to his toes and summoning all his arm strength, he hurls the rock toward the mine entrance. It falls short of its mark and clatters harmlessly out of sight. Pleased with his symbolic act of defiance, he smiles, turns to retrace his steps and begins whistling to mute the angry sounds behind him.

No trails mark passage through the dense stand of second-growth firs and spruce before him, and the forest humus reveals no footprints. But he knows his way. He's eleven years old, and he's not afraid to travel alone in the Klamath forests. On weekends his father mostly has too many accumulated home chores for the two to enjoy an outing together, and his mother grades papers and prepares for the next week's classes. Sometimes his school chums join him, but mostly they have other pressing interests. They don't understand their friend's attraction to the Klamath's least-trod paths. "You're just playing Indian again," they tease. He's accustomed to going companionless. He savors solitude. Accommodating others is a burden, and he's pleased to be free from it.

An hour later he scrambles up and over two lichen-covered boulders nearly the size of his school bus. Pressing against his chest are dusky-green rock faces mottled in bright crimson. What did his father say about them? Yes, he remembers. "Serpentine rocks of the Klamath. Blood rocks we call them. Each one preserves a Hupok's blood drained into it at death." He shudders as somber images crowd into his mind.

The blood rocks channel an outlet from his secluded pool. When he discovered the pool a week ago, the creek raged high and milky from heavy rains. Then he couldn't see into the pool, but watched in awe as two steelhead tried again and again to leap the cascade roaring from its outlet. Side-by-side and propelled by powerful tails, the pair surged four feet nearly straight up against the flow, only to fall back inches short from the top. He was sure he watched a mated pair who had followed the rain-swollen creek far from its mother river to return to their ancestral spawning beds. He clapped his hands in approval when the two fish finally succeeded in their ascent and disappeared from sight into the pool's murky depths.

Now, a week without rain has lowered Indian Creek by over a foot, and its tributaries ripple into the pool clear and untroubled. Too impatient to find a place to sit, he remains standing, retrieves his lunch, wolfs it down, returns the candy bar wrapper to his shirt pocket, and restuffs the newspaper and apple core inside the back of his shirt. Swiping at his mouth with a hand, he approaches the smaller inlet. Although he's anxious to see if the fish are still there, caution prevails and he crawls the last few feet on his belly. Clammy streamside grasses add a lingering winter chill to his sweat-dampened shirt. He shivers, first when the cold penetrates to his skin, then again when full-length body contact with the earth triggers his sense of natural kinship to all living things.

He looks into the pool, but sees nothing. Pausing to quench his thirst, he's careful to minimize disturbance, strains as far forward as he dares, and sucks water directly from the surface. Then, to improve his vision angle, he rises to his elbows and stares before him. His mirrored reflection stares back. A youth's insouciant smile betrays his mood and denies the more somber image of serious and penetrating gray eyes. Bright red and green beads on his headband glint in the sunlight. His long black hair, only partly restrained by the band, flows beyond his reflection. He adjusts his hawk's feather so it juts forward from his headband at a comical angle, as if it grows from his head. He laughs and sticks out his tongue. A playful likeness responds in kind. Then, as if to punish him, a rogue ray of light glares off the surface and momentarily blinds him. He blinks and shuts his eyes for a few seconds, until the searing white orb behind his lids finally fades. When he opens his eyes, he squints and peers deeper into the pool.

Two dark, torpedo-shaped forms ease from the depths toward him and stop below the inlet. Except for a barely perceptible fanning of their fins, they hold motionless. Fearing he might startle them with movement, he suppresses an urge to clap his hands again. He's sure it's the same pair from the week before. One of the fish is smaller and crimson sided. Its lower jaw curls into a menacing, hooked end. *The cockfish*, he thinks. The other is larger with swollen, silvery sides. *Has to be the hen. Full of eggs.*

He studies the creek-bed above the hovering fish. *Ah-h, yes, their nest...a redd, Papa called it.* The redd is three feet across where the fish have brushed aside sediment to uncover the stream's pebbled bottom. He looks closer. Green and lilac gravel glint back at him. From his father's descriptions, he realizes that he is admiring small deposits of pure jade. Glittering remnants of an ancestral lode that once connected to the outcropping below have now been exposed by sweeping fishtails. Soon, the gravel will host spawn of a generation bearing the legacy of death but also providing a promise of birth for a new generation.

Although he's sure they haven't seen him, the fish are skittish. They race to their nest, then drift warily back into the shadows of deeper water. Several times they streak through the shallows, as if chased. The pool surface V's behind them in long, rippling wakes, then erupts in a noisy splash when they suddenly turn. He watches the hen breach twice in front of him. She leaps free from the water and belly-flops back, slapping the surface with a loud clap. *Loosening her egg sacks, just like Papa said.*

The process repeats again, and then shadows from overhead obscure his view. Twisting his head, he scowls up at a darkened sky. Clouds are building, stealing the light he needs to see what's happening beneath the surface. Is a storm coming? He knows he must leave—now.

Sighing, he rises and begins retracing his steps. As he approaches the blood rocks, he feels both a chill and a foreboding. A glimpse into his future? Again he shudders and pauses to pull on his sweater. Once below the ominous serpentine faces, he stops and shakes his head and shoulders, as if to free himself from an unpleasant burden. Troubling images leave. Now warmer both inside and out, he smiles and removes his sweater, knotting it around his neck.

Feeling a familiar exhilaration that comes from using gravity as an ally, he abandons caution and hurries his pace—faster and faster, until he's running, leaping fallen logs, dodging boulders, swiping away bushes and branches that reach out and try to ensnarl him. When the way forward steepens, he disdains an easier switch-backing descent and a safer, slower pace. Instead, keeping both feet together, he begins to jump—out and down, out and down, way out and way down. He dares gravity to release him into the sky or bring him crashing to earth. Only when he must either slow his speed or stumble and fall does he brace his feet and come skidding to a stop.

Sooner than he thought possible, he emerges from the last forest grove and approaches the Paladora. Chest heaving and breathing in gasps, he sprints the final few yards to his bicycle. Silence greets him. He's pleased that the miners are gone, and he imagines that his rock throw scared them away. On impulse he faces the old Douglas fir, salutes it, cranes his neck and lets his gaze wander up the length of it, up into its highest reaches. There three slender spires of new growth defy destiny and thrust their future promise into the freedom of the sky.

THE next Saturday, he again risks a supperless evening as he stays late at the confluence pool. He watches the hen deposit cluster after cluster of hundreds of tiny golden eggs within the ring of the redd. He's fascinated by the frantic body spasms and contortions of the male, who rushes in behind his mate and squirts her eggs with a milky white fluid. He wonders if the reproduction process is all the agony it appears, either for steelhead, most of whom he knows will die after the effort, or for other species. From the comments of older boys at school, he gathers the process is more pleasurable for humans and will become the object of intense preoccupation as boys and girls grow older.

A WEEK later, the fish are gone. He wonders if someone caught them. Why anyone would want to capture a wild thing during its mission of replenishment is an enigma to him. Then the Indian side of his mind reminds him that steelhead were a vital food source that helped sustain his ancestors for many generations.

He's still troubled when he returns home. He waits for his father to finish an after-dinner pipe and asks, "What happened to the fish, Papa? They didn't die after spawning. I saw no remains. And, they weren't caught. I saw no tracks there but my own."

"They'll try to return to the sea," his father explains. "But it's over a hundred miles and they're very weak. Most will die in the attempt; only a few will succeed."

"Do you think my pair will make it to the sea?"

"Perhaps."

"I hope so. If they do, will they come back next year?"

"Yes."

"To the same pool?"

"Yes. They will try. It's a rare thing, but it is possible. In years to come, their descendants will follow."

IN summer he returns to the spawning pool whenever he tires of pursuing his relentless upstream curiosity. He watches schools of fingerlings grow to several inches in length by autumn. Once he throws stones at a pair of kingfishers who brazenly poach the hordes of tiny fish. "Fly away!" he screams at them. The angry birds perch out of range and scold him for interrupting their meal. Then, suddenly, the fingerlings all disappear to begin their long and perilous journey to the sea.

HE thrills to see his spawning pair return the following March. But the year after, his long Saturday excursions and solitary vigils go unrewarded. The pool is barren and remains so the following year. Why descendants of the original pair don't find their way back to the spawning pool and continue the spawning cycle is a river mystery the boy yearns to solve. When he hears reports of similar spawning failures throughout the Klamath system, he asks his father about them.

"The wild strains of Klamath steelhead are disappearing," his father tells him. "They spawn too high in our mountains. Logging ruins their spawning beds. Removing so many trees destroys the earth's natural glue, and loosened soil washes into the streams and covers the redds with silt. The river's tributaries lose their protection from the sun, and unshaded streams warm and shrink. Wherever the white man goes, he litters. His debris chokes our stream channels. His mines poison our water. His diversions reduce our streams to impassable trickles. Fishermen over-harvest the pools when our streams are low. Steelhead are easy prey then, as they hold and rest, waiting for rains to bring the fresh surge of water they need to continue upstream. Hunters drive our game higher and higher into the mountains to survive. But our fish find less and less sanctuary there. Without access to their ancestral spawning grounds, our native steelhead runs will disappear."

"Someday, will we learn how to save our wild fish?" The boy asks.

"Perhaps." And then his father shakes his head. "But I don't think so. First the white man will have to overcome his need for another kill and his urge to exploit the riches found in our mountains, streams, and forests. And it's not in a white man's nature to deny greed for such a simple thing as a fish."

OWANDAGA
Night of the Sleeping Moon

*T*HE MAN PARKS AND CONCEALS his van where he'd left his bicycle forty-five years before. He walks back and covers his tire tracks so the road shows no sign of his exit. He listens and hears only natural forest sounds. He knows the jade mine is gone, its riches all harvested years before. He doesn't miss its presence.

When he looks back along the road just traveled, familiar warmth swells inside him. *It feels the same,* he thinks. *It's still the Paladora to me. It still fills me with the pride of my father's people, even though there are no Hupoks left here to travel the Paladora with me.* He shakes his head and sighs. *All gone. They're all gone. All the old Hupoks are gone from this part of the Klamath. Like my father, all dead. And their children, if any survive, are but shameful remnants of a once proud race, living on the reservation in poverty or lost in the white man's world and wandering aimlessly with the winds. No one remembers the pathway to the sun, what it was like before it became just another dusty road to nowhere, eventually swallowed by our impassive Klamath mountains.* He sighs again.

This evening his mission differs from his boyhood quests, but his route remains initially the same. He'll stay with Indian Creek until he reaches the confluence pool. Then he'll veer east and climb steeply uphill to the high benches of Doolittle Creek, where, many years earlier, the timber companies clear-cut a vast area. Replacement growth has developed an extensive natural canopy, and now the old logging tracts provide ideal plantation

sites where marijuana growers tend their crops, secluded deep
inside the national forest.

An hour later, breathing heavily, he stands beside the familiar confluence pool. Its shadowed surface is undisturbed. He
looks up and watches heaven's illustrator abandon a colorless
midsummer sunset in the west and perform in the east a different metamorphosis of color and light. Powers of transformation
are displayed as dramatically at day's end as at day's beginning.
Nature's shade operates inversely, as last rays of sunlight retreat
from hilltops and disappear into the eastern horizon. Diffused
light tints the darkening sky, first with pinks and lavenders, then
with indigos and soul-scorching deep magentas, liberating all the
secret shades of the spectrum's most elusive colors. *Mora is contrary tonight. The Sun God paints his canvas on the other side of the
evening sky.*

He turns then to the west, anticipating the brief wind flurry
occurring at sunset of a windless day. He feels soft breezes, like
sighs of the mountain spirits, cool his cheek and strengthen his
resolve. He wipes sweat from his forehead with the back of his
forearm. Running his hands through a clump of dried bunch
grass, he strips bright yellow seed pods from their purple stems,
absently sifts desiccated grains through his fingers, and sprinkles
them on the ground. When he scans the pool's protective rim of
rock outcroppings, he sees that their lichen colonies, once mul-
ticolored patchworks of black, silver, green, orange, and yellow,
are shredded and parched to a common shade of dull olive drab.
Good, the high forests will be dry too.

Impatience pushes at him, but he suppresses the impulse to
hurry on. He looks up at the darkening sky. *Still too early.* Then
memory tugs at him, and he returns his gaze to the pool. Out
of curiosity he peers into the depths before him. Barely enough
light remains for him to see beneath the surface. Nothing moves
there. He hasn't expected anything. Then silvery flashes catch
the corner of his eye, and he looks across the pool to its shallows. Iridescent in failing light, a school of fingerlings rushes back
and forth in the shadows. He smiles. He's surprised he didn't

notice them the month before. After all these years, a pair of steelhead has obviously returned. Somehow they've overcome all of man's obstacles, once again traveled high into Indian Creek's drainage, and successfully spawned. He wonders if they might be wild fish, maybe descended from the pair he watched here so long ago. More likely they're offspring of hatchery plantings. But still an encouragement for his future? The thrill of seeing a renewed presence of river life in the confluence pool sends a tremor through him. *Could it be a sign? A sign of renewed hope for the river? Renewed hope for me?*

Sighing, he lies on his back, gathers strength and purpose from his contact with earth, and watches the sky. He looks to the heavens for first starlight. No moon will light his way tonight. Only the stars. He's purposely selected the month's darkest night. Owandaga, night of the sleeping moon, the Hupoks called it. He needs protection of dark more than he needs additional light. He knows his way without a moon. During his two years in the growers' camps, he learned well the plantations' topographies. He'll need the instinctive stealth of his most renowned forebears tonight. The growers increase their guards after each burning, and this is his third mission of the year. He hopes the growers haven't yet associated his arsons with the night of the new moon. When they do, he knows they'll be waiting for him.

He knows he takes enormous risk. He accepts it, welcomes it. His risk increases with each Owandaga mission. Even if he escapes detection by the guards, there are still workers in the camps who know him. If any see him, the word will spread, and the growers will come for him. The hunter will become the hunted.

So far he's been careful—and lucky. Careful because he plans well, eschews collaboration, and takes no unnecessary chances. Lucky because no mistakes flaw his carefulness. And he's successful because he burns with a crusader's zeal for justice. For him, government justice and enforcement systems move too slowly. National forest officials complain they don't have the staff or training to eradicate the growers; the state contends plantations on the national forest are out of state jurisdiction; and, although they deny it, local law enforcement is afraid to confront the illicit activities.

He closes his eyes and visualizes a small burial plot and the grave of his last born, there where she rests beside his parents. He digs his fingers into the soil beneath him as if to vent painful memories. He renews his solemn vow of retribution to the mountain spirits. After all these years, hunger for vengeance still consumes him. *By the Gods of my Hupok ancestors, I'll burn the growers out if it takes a lifetime.* No one knows of his oft-repeated vow. He confides in no one, not even Doreen or their surviving daughter. No one counsels him. He keeps his anger to himself. Let others talk. He will act.

It's dark when he finally rises. Fear knots his belly. Fear isn't a stranger, but fear is no longer an unwelcome companion. This fear is different from the one before. This fear will keep him alert. His shoulders ache and his legs feel leaden. *Maybe I rested too long.* He rubs his legs, wishing the Gods would return to him the stamina of youth—for just a few more nights. But he knows they won't. The strength of purpose he carries in his mind will have to give him what he needs to complete his mission.

From a hidden cache beneath a natural rock cluster, he retrieves a small pack containing his incendiary materials. He checks his shirt pocket for two fresh chocolate bars, pulls a black cotton cap down over his ears, fills a canteen with fresh water from the pool and dabs poolside mud on his forehead, nose, cheeks, and chin. Then, grimacing with pain, he shoulders his pack and moves away from the confluence pool, its starlit banks and its time-faded memories. Maintaining a soundless passage, he enters the shadowed forest beyond, limping slightly. As he stalks among the evergreens and through fern groves, he listens to the brawling clamor of Indian Creek ebb to a constant murmur behind him. He nods his head to acknowledge that he's heard the ghosts of his ancestors whisper their approval.

Soon he's just another faint shadow in the night.

PRIDE

GROGGY FROM BARELY an hour's sleep, Charlie groaned at the noises—*V-R-R-R-OOM, V-R-R-R-OOM, V-R-R-R-OOM.* Raging and insistent, they clamored through an open window and assaulted him. He shook his head and stuffed it under his pillow. The familiar sounds diminished but wouldn't go away—*v-r-r-r-oom, v-r-r-r-oom, v-r-r-r-oom.* Too well he knew the source of his torment—the first logging truck roaring down Huckleberry Mountain—and the consequences he would have to endure. *A specter from my past haunts me with images from long ago.* Every day it woke him up at dawn. No relief, not even on this special morning, the morning after a moonless night, when a nocturnal mission more important than sleep commanded his attention.

He knew a second truck would follow in five minutes. And a third five minutes after that. On a good day, twelve trucks screamed out of the Marble Mountains every hour until sunset. The drivers gunned their huge Peterbilts fast along Fryingpan Ridge, and their straining engines filled the valley with furious sounds. Then, like shrieks from some forest demon denying the leash, air brakes squealed and ravaged what was left of natural voices. Downshifting gears screeched in protest as the drivers fought to control their trucks and swing them into a long, treacherous curve turning off the ridge and onto a cliff-side highway 100 feet above the river. One miscalculation here and the Klamath gulped another expensive rig, belched forth a load of fresh-cut logs, most of which were salvaged down-river, and claimed another life whose soul defied salvage. "The river forgives few mistakes," his father once told him. "Respect the Klamath, but don't fear it. And don't tempt it. Honor it and it will sustain you. Disdain it and it will destroy you."

Charlie groaned again. He tried to relax his mind, but he couldn't. *Why am I so affected by sounds? When I was a boy, sounds always brought fanciful images. Now they only bring memories, all the old memories: first pride, then fear…and finally shame. Always ending with shame.*

"Forgive yourself and forget…I have," Doreen tried to reassure him when his shame got so bad he had to talk about it or explode. Although he'd finally forgiven himself, he still couldn't forget. Never would he forget. Not while those damned trucks forced his past into his earliest thoughts each morning. *Will they never finish logging the Marble Mountains, move on and leave me in peace?* He banged his fist on the wooden floor, placed his palms on each side of his head, and squeezed—hard, trying to force out memories flooding his consciousness. Then he relaxed, sighed, and accepted the inevitable, knowing his first memories would be good ones—from his pride years.

When he closed his eyes, three decades disappeared, and he smiled as he saw himself young, strong, and invincible, a logging-truck driver, the best on the river.

———————

AS USUAL, he wakes up refreshed from only five hours sleep and welcomes pre-dawn stillness, eager to begin a new day. *Good. I'll be gone before first birds sing.* Soft light from a crescent moon seeps through the west window and flows into their bedroom. Bathed in serenity, Doreen's face still nestles against his shoulder. He senses her approaching wakefulness, and he reaches over to deliver a caress, hesitates…*she needs her sleep*…and then resists the urge to engage in morning intimacy. *Time for that later.* Carefully he separates from her.

That other urge, the urge to get going, is strong inside him.

As it is every morning. *Why am I so obsessed? It's only work. No day off in nearly a month now.* For twenty-five straight days, he's been first in line to unload at the Wooley Creek Mill. Being first is his own expectation of himself. Being first brings him a sense of accomplishment he tried to explain to Doreen the night before.

SHE'D asked him why he was so obsessed. He'd shaken his head and said, "I'm not sure."

"You're just being competitive," she said.

"No, there's more to it."

"More what?" she demanded, teasing him with her eyes.

He struggled with an answer. "I don't know. Pride, maybe. Is that a bad thing?"

"No, Charlie the Hawk. That's your mind at work. Mind pride is a good thing."

Still he struggled—for a more complete explanation. "Am I just proud that I'm young and strong, proud that I can drive with the best?"

She laughed. "Oh-h-h, Tamiko, you *are* the best." Then she captured his hands with hers. "Both here..." as she squeezed his hands "...and here..." as she placed his hands against his chest, over his heart.

SMILING with the recollection, he sits up and gazes at the moon through the window. Heavy dew has condensed overnight, formed droplets and now begins to streak the window pane. *Big rain coming?* Still careful not to disturb Doreen, he rises and moves across the room, wincing at contact of his bare feet with the cold floor. Recovering his clothes from the chair where he threw them the night before, he dresses quickly, wincing again as chill, damp underwear connects with his skin. *Fresh sock day,* he remembers. Returning to the bed, he retrieves a heavy pair of woolen socks from the nightstand. He puts them on without sitting, awkwardly hopping first on one foot and then the other, like a marionette dancing on a string.

Hearing Doreen stir and then nestle into the warm depression his body has just vacated, he turns and watches her curl up with her knees beneath her chin and her arms encircling his pillow as if to hold him captive to her dreams. Now unable to resist touching her...*this caretaker of my heart*...he kneels beside her and gently dishevels her hair, separating it into long strands with his fingers until it covers his pillow like a fine silken mantle. He strokes her cheek, then presses his lips to the exposed ear and whispers, "Bye, river creature."

With her eyes still closed, Doreen smiles, then sighs, crinkles her nose, bats at him with her hand like a kitten, and mumbles, "Bye, Hawk. Be safe. Please be safe." Then she burrows deeper into the enclave retaining his body heat and murmurs, "Eat a proper breakfast, but please put your boots on outside and don't turn on a light."

He lingers at bedside and chuckles at her drowsy fight against wakefulness. He feels it then, the day's first feeling, a powerful warmth surging from deep inside—a feeling of pride in others, his heart pride. He knows this pride well and savors it. It's a selfless pride that nurtures happiness, kindles passion, and keeps love fresh and genuine—a spontaneous pride that wells naturally from his heart without needing conscious effort.

His heart swells again when he steps into his daughters' windowless bedroom. Michele and Carleen are still sleeping and will until sunrise. In night's darkest hour he can barely see them, but he hears their untroubled breathing from the bunk beds he built for them. He pads over in stocking feet. Conceding her elder sister's preemptive right to the higher sleeping station, Carleen occupies the lower bunk. A restless sleeper—"The Thrasher," Doreen calls her—Carleen, as usual, has shaken her blanket to the floor during the night. He stoops to recover and replace it. Then he confirms that Michele has indeed, as usual, pulled up her blanket and top sheet until they leave her bare feet exposed. Resisting a temptation to tickle her feet, he adjusts her blanket, brushes her cheek with his lips, and then stoops again to repeat the same soft caress for Carleen. They don't stir. "Bye, kids," he whispers. "Verancora." He uses the Hupok word for "daughters of my heart."

PRE-DAWN darkness, drowsy silence and a damp chill greet him as he leaves the house. One hand clasps his old school lunch box and his new rain slicker. A long-handled flashlight swings from the other. Warmth suffuses his feet and ankles—from corked logging boots that absorbed heat from the wood cook-stove as he finished breakfast. Their worn metal nubs scrunch against loose driveway gravel as he strides to his truck, whistling cheerfully. He focuses his flashlight beam on the door, where Doreen's bold artistry displays *Charlie's Pride,* in scripted letters emblazoned in black on a bright red shield. As he swings into the cab, he feels another familiar warmth, this one springing from a different internal source, the one Doreen diagnosed. He acknowledges his mind pride is a conscious self-esteem, a cultivated knowledge of self-worth, born of aspiration and validated by accomplishment, bringing him a sense of satisfaction without conceit. It's a pride that sometimes challenges modesty and flirts with vanity, but remains honest.

As if to say, "Okay, Boss, I'm ready if you're ready. Let's go haul logs," the truck's engine fires smoothly at first press on the starter, and he nods his head in approval.

WITH his truck fully loaded on his first run, he accelerates to top speed in a long straight stretch of empty highway. Through morning mists steaming from the pavement he races, daring to deny a relentless pursuit from the rising sun. Fresh-cut logs—several tons of them—jostle just behind him, daring him to hesitate or slow down. When he finally slows into a curve, he smiles in anticipation. Looming ahead is a dilapidated tavern, a niche of dubious humanity nestled between a wild river and the narrow strip of pavement daring to tame it. A Klamath fixture for decades, Tony Fisheyes is a local favorite for food and drink. Yes, as he expected, six rigs from Tony's breakfast crowd are there, parked in elongated gravel parking strips that extend more than a hundred feet from the tavern in each direction. He watches the rigs grow larger and larger, each with its pair of tandem eight-wheeled trailers, one stacked on top of the other. Soon the tavern appears trapped in the center of a swarm of giant and grotesque metallic creatures still sleeping in their mating ritual's last embrace.

Eating, talking, and drinking coffee when they should be driving, he thinks. He laughs and gives the late-rising drivers one long, disdainful blast from his horn as he passes. He knows they recognize who taunts them, knows they curse him for being so early with the first run, but also knows they concede that at daybreak Highway 96 belongs to the Hawk. "How does it feel to own the dawn?" Doreen teased him the night before. He challenged, "Get up some day. Come feel it with me." She crinkled her nose at him when she replied, "No-o-o thank you, Hawk. Much too early for me."

AT midday and into his second run, he feels his mind pride surge again where the highway descends to a shadowless river at an old barge crossing. A solitary drift boat at the edge of the Klamath captures his peripheral vision. Its sole occupant holds his oars motionless and dripping above the surface, floating as if attached to the river without separately identifiable movement, seeming without purpose. Charlie tries to guess which river traveler is also earliest risen and also first to Golddiggers' Ford. He greets the river's paradigm with two brash toots on his horn, and the fisherman who owns the waterway dawn acknowledges his recognition of the driver who owns the roadway dawn by dropping his oars and flapping his arms to imitate the wings of a hawk rushing in flight.

NEAR day's end, he hurtles downriver toward a blinding sunset, his eyes blurring with fatigue. As he approaches his log home, he squints to clear his vision and honks his special message, three quick beeps followed by a repetition. His home is barely visible through the trees, but he knows Doreen will recognize he's on his third and final run. He can't see them, but he knows two small children are racing to the window to wave as their father passes. His heart pride swells again, suffuses him with warmth, and drives away his arm and shoulder fatigue. He slows, downshifts, and then accelerates to let his family hear the roar of his engine and the blast from its exhaust—the exultant song of *Charlie's Pride* in full voice.

Then he's gone. He knows Doreen will eat dinner with the girls and save a plate for him. Before he eats, he'll complete a nightly ritual—wash down his truck, and fulfill his nightly promise to Michele and Carleen. With him leading and all of them skipping, chattering, and laughing, he'll escort his daughters to bed, tuck them in, and then read to them from his *Calvin and Hobbes* collection. Now, he still has two hours of driving ahead of him, time to savor his prides—and his two enduring passions, for the river that flows beside him and for the family waiting patiently for his return.

WHEN he finally switches off the ignition, he breathes deeply and feels tension drain from him as his internal engine also shuts down. Darkness has claimed his surroundings and obscures the outlines of his home. *How seldom I get to see it in daylight.* He closes his eyes and enjoys a brief period of rest and silence, an actual break, his first in sixteen hours. Fatigue captures his body, but his mind escapes and creates an image of Doreen and his daughters waiting for him, hearing his truck approach, and, when the engine ceased, racing to the front door to greet him. His heart pride swells again. He's a man at peace, basking in a powerful and sustaining connection to his time and place. Safely secluded from a very public world, with all its instability and all its flaws, he rejoices in his private domain of permanence and perfection.

When he opens his eyes, a different and long-forgotten image intrudes—sitting at the dinner table, his parents discussing his dual heritage. This image challenges his sense of well being, allows doubt an incursion into his thoughts. *Have I followed nei-*

ther heritage and thereby failed in both? He shakes his head to rid
himself of uncertainty, shrugs his shoulders, and reaches for the
door handle to his truck.

———————

ROARING ENGINES AND squealing brakes again intruded
and returned his mind to the present. Many times over the inter-
vening years, Charlie had asked himself the same self-condemning
question about honoring his duality, an answer for which he'd
always avoided. Not now. *Yes,* he acknowledged, *I've failed both
heritages. But redemption is yet possible. It's not too late.*

A body still aching from the night before collaborated with
truck noises to keep him awake. Stubbornly he fought against rising so early. This time he forced his memory to drift him back in
time. He needed to revisit his pride years again. But he wouldn't
let fear or shame back in. Not this morning. Not after last
night.

Hell, yes, he'd been proud during those years. On most days
he'd delivered three loads. You had to be the best to deliver three
loads. Downriver to the Wooley Creek Mill was sixty miles, more
when the timber companies logged deeper in the forest. Highway
96 twisted and turned all the way as it followed the river's serpentine course: long sinuous curves, single and double S turns,
abrupt right-angle bends. He knew them all, all 187 of them.
He'd counted them. You had to be a helluva driver to master the
turns and deliver three loads a day, pushing your rig hard to the
mill and then harder yet—to the limit—back upriver to wait in
line like a taxi driver for another load.

And you had to have special skills. Lots of them. Skill in placing the load chains to be sure you didn't lose logs, or a whole
load, in the turns. Skill in knowing where you could pass tourist cars, granny drivers the truckers called them, and where you
couldn't, and knowing how fast you could push a rig when rainwater ran an inch deep on the highway and your wipers, even at
full speed, couldn't clear the windshield. Skill in knowing when
a balding tire was only a hundred miles from blowout and in

recognizing when an overstressed engine screamed in agony for overhaul or death. And skill in downshifting tired gears when you ran too fast downhill and couldn't afford new brakes until next month.

And you had to have instinctive steering in the turns. You needed that invisible guide controlling the wheel, telling you when to slow, when you could speed up, warning you when the maw of the river was about to suck you off a curve.

Most of all, you had to have nerves incorruptible by hazard, time, or fatigue.

He knew he'd had it all: skill, instinct, and implacable nerves. "The Hawk has nerves like Klamath granite," the other drivers said.

And the loggers, each with his special talent—faller, bucker, choker setter, high climber, until technology made him obsolete—had to work fast to keep pace with the drivers. Waiting drivers revved their engines impatiently, leaned out their windows and yelled at the burly loggers, "Hurry up you witless mules. We've got a big truck mortgage to pay and bankers who never wait." The loggers feigned unconcern, leaned on their equipment to rest and yelled back, "Don't rile your hemorrhoids. Come on down here, you butt-sitting leeches. Come down here and do some real work!" But both loggers and drivers knew they needed each other, and you had to be sure you didn't forget it.

And you needed to be lucky. Yes, lucky too. Being lucky meant bad weather didn't turn too awful on the days you drove. It meant your rig didn't go down for repairs too often. It meant you didn't get too sick or too hung-over—or too afraid—to drive. If you were lucky and could deliver three loads a day, you could pay off a rig in three years. Then you could make big, debt-free money for another two years before you replaced your rig and began the cycle again.

Enough of the past. Charlie finally conceded to the sounds of commerce and accepted it was time to get out of bed. He sat up and then grimaced at the stiffness in his legs when he stood up. *Damn arthritis, a curse from the present.* A rising sun directed a ray of light through the window toward him. The sudden flood of sunshine chased away his mind shadows and bathed him in hopeful expectation. A day off was before him. All those undone things around his cabin would have to wait. He was going fishing—just for himself, something he hadn't done in a long time. Maybe he'd also stop to rest at a Klamath island, take a nap even, something else he hadn't done in a very long time.

FEAR

V-R-R-R-OOM, V-R-R-R-OOM, V-R-R-R-OOM. There they were again, more effective than an alarm clock. Charlie shuddered. After a day off to fish and rest, he still felt unprepared to endure the invasion of pre-dawn truck sounds—and their consequences. *Damn.* Again he pounded his fists on the floor. *Body rested, but mind still in turmoil.* His thoughts drifted back and forth in time. *I was luckier than most,* he acknowledged. *I drove through four cycles and part of a fifth…twenty-two years. A helluva lot longer than most. How many miles? Maybe two million. I wore out four trucks. And then my nerves wore out. Granite turned to sponge and fear sopped in. For all those years I kept fear at bay, and then I couldn't resist it anymore. Then there was never enough beer and whiskey to keep night fears away, never enough sleep to prevent day fears from greeting me when I awoke.*

Memories pounded away at the doorway to his mind. They created a mental ache impervious to will or medication. *Better I should facilitate memories rather than suppress them? Maybe if I relive fear just one more time, it won't keep returning to haunt me.* He closed his eyes, again opened his mind, and turned the memory pages back ten years.

AS USUAL, HE'S awake and has risen early, but a fearful reluctance to leave home in darkness keeps him immobile. Like a paralysis, it holds him captive to the warmth of the woodstove.

As dawn absorbs night and extinguishes the stars, soft gray light filters into the kitchen where he remains motionless. He sits with his eyes open, seeing nothing, his shoulders slumped in dejection, his head sunken so low his chin nearly touches his chest. His long, silver-streaked hair, usually well-groomed in its natural state, now hangs uncombed and unkempt. His chair-back rests against the table, where a half-eaten bowl of oatmeal has grown cold. When he finally stirs and reaches for his boots, his body shakes as from a sudden chill, despite warmth still radiating from the stove before him. He curses his inability to control trembling fingers, and he has difficulty lacing his boots.

Can't let Doreen see me like this. I have to go...go now...have to drive today. With a supreme effort of will, he lurches to his feet, reaches to the counter for his lunch pail and shuffles unsteadily out of the kitchen. Pausing, he hears her stirring in the bedroom behind him. He doesn't look back, but over his shoulder he mumbles a faint, "Bye, river creature."

SMOKE from the mill's three stacks hangs suspended above the Klamath like a long, sickly cloud trapped in the gorge. At each bend permitting him a downriver view, he watches as the brown-tinged white blanket grows larger and larger until it spreads for several miles above and below Wooley Creek. Slowly it creeps up the hillsides like a loathsome killing fog banished from the river. Mill smoke means he's late again in delivering his first load. *At least fear is also late.*

Anxiety reclaims him as he slows to a stop, seventh truck in line at the mill's offloading dock. Confinement to his truck cab becomes unbearable. Moving awkwardly he steps out. Rubbing his hands against stiffness in his arms and shoulders, he paces around his truck—again and again. *Will that line never move forward?*

Like a shroud, gloom envelops him, half external, from the damp mill-haze that sunshine struggles to penetrate, and half internal, from the nameless apprehension tormenting him. He can think of nothing beyond how fearful and agitated he feels. He has to unload and leave—soon, before…before what? He can't identify what he needs to run from. That his anxiety's source is unknown only increases his terror. He pounds his fists against the engine's cowling, until his hands are bruised, cut and bleeding. *Gotta wear gloves to protect me from myself. At least fear retreats when I have physical pain to endure.*

"WHAT'S the matter, Hawk?" Doreen asks him that night, when his fear erupts again. "You're sweating like a bucker in midsummer."

He forces his words through clenched teeth. "It's the fear, Doreen. The goddam fear. I'm always afraid."

"Afraid of what?"

"I don't know. The rig. The road. The river. Maybe I'm afraid I'll miss a curve."

"You've never missed one yet. And you sure don't miss them in bed either," she purrs. "Come, Tamiko. Come drive my curves. I'll drive away your fear." Doreen snuggles closer to him.

"Nothing drives it away, Doreen. Nothing." He sits up and holds his face in his hands. He can't bear to look at her, let her see the suffering in his eyes. "Not your curves. Not whiskey. Not sleep. Not fishing the river. Not talking. Not anything." Now his entire body is trembling, and he curses his inability to control it. He rises from bed and stumbles to a window. There he gazes into a moonless, star-filled sky. Its brilliance clusters in the Milky Way like a celestial sash of diamonds. "Not even the peaceful stillness I once loved in our Klamath nights," he mumbles into the windowpane.

She rises on one elbow. Her eyes follow him and fill with concern. "Why are you afraid?"

"I don't know."

"There must be a reason."

"Too many birthdays? Too many miles? I just don't know."

"Tell me about your fear, Charlie."

The stoic Indian side of his mind resists conversation about a feeling as shameful as fear. Difficult to acknowledge, impossible to talk about. When he finally responds, he's unable to turn away from the window and face her. His voice is that of a beaten man in pain, his words strained and halting, "I'm not sure I can. How do I explain my fear? Something I don't understand? Something that makes me feel ashamed...too ashamed to talk about it?"

"Try, Charlie. Try. I know you're a brave man. How does a brave man know fear?"

"As a stranger? Like I'm a stranger to fear."

"Are you?"

"I don't know...maybe this fear doesn't belong with me. It's a treacherous fear...it sneaks up on me when I don't expect it... when it doesn't make sense for me to be afraid."

"And you're not making sense."

"I know. I'm not afraid when I should be afraid. It's not a fear of the moment. I'm not afraid when I'm driving. When I'm in the truck, I'm too busy braking and shifting gears in the turns, too busy accelerating at just the right instant, making sure I can feel the highway through my hands on the steering wheel. I don't wear gloves like the other drivers, and when I drive I'm too busy reacting to the feel of the highway to feel fear. But fear must be there in the back of my mind. Fear is a predator waiting to pounce on me if my concentration falters or I try and relax."

She rises from the bed and walks to the window to stand behind him. She massages his neck and shoulder muscles, feeling knots inside. Then she encircles his waist with her arms and rests her head in the curve between his shoulder blades. "Are you afraid now?" she asks.

"Yes. May the Gods help me. Yes, I'm afraid. Even now."

She feels his body tremble, but remains silent and increases the pressure of her embrace.

"Fear sneaks up on me," he continues. "It stalks me when I'm waiting for a load, when I'm at the mill waiting to unload, and even in the evening when I'm trying to read or tie flies. It lets me sleep, but then it ambushes me when I wake up in the morning."

"And your dreams? Does fear torment your dreams?"

"No. And I don't understand that either. I don't have fear in my dreams, only when I'm awake. It's a conscious fear but not a specific fear. It's a general fright. It freezes my body. I feel like I can't do anything. It captures my mind so I can't think of anything except how afraid I am. I'm just afraid."

"Of?"

"Everything. I'm afraid to do anything."

"That doesn't make any sense either."

"I know. That's part of the terror. When I ask myself what I'm afraid of, I don't have a good answer. I think I'm afraid of driving, but I don't know what I'm afraid will happen if I drive. Have an accident? Or, maybe I'm afraid my nerves are gone, and I won't be able to drive, won't be able to support my family. I'm not sure. There are no visions to help me. If it was a specific fear, I could fight it. But I don't know what to fight. I wonder if I fear the river. But, isn't the river supposed to be my friend? Is the Klamath waiting for me to make a mistake? Why? I don't know. Is it some kind of stupid Indian fear, a superstitious fear? Or is it from that other part of me, some kind of white man's fear my Indian side can't comprehend? I just don't know."

Again she tightens her embrace. "You're so tense, Hawk. I can feel the tension inside you when I touch you. And it doesn't go away when I hold you, try to comfort you."

"Maybe I've spent too many years ignoring the tension, refusing to acknowledge it. Now there's too much held back and it overflows. It comes raging through me like a noxious, uncontrollable virus. It squeezes my chest until I can't breathe. It sends a blood rush through me. My muscles tremble as if they know they must do something, but don't know what. Then I breathe too fast and my heart beats too fast, and that makes me frightened of what fear is doing to me. My fear is a monster that feeds on itself."

"So...so, what are we...what are you going to do?"

"I don't know. I just don't know."

"Charlie, you've got to do something. You're miserable with the fear. And you're driving me crazy...because I don't know how to help you. Even our daughters know something is wrong. What do other drivers do?"

"I've seen them when their fear gets unmanageable. They drink too much and their livers go bad. Or they quit driving. Or they make a mistake, run their rigs off the highway and end up food for the big schools of immature fish in the river."

"Well, you're sure drinking too much. I don't like you stopping at Tony Fisheyes before you come home at night. You never used to do that. I know you think the beer or whiskey will ease your pain. But it frightens me."

He's silent for a moment. She releases her embrace and they turn away from the window. They face each other then, and he takes her hands in his. "Maybe I should quit driving." His voice is subdued, hesitant.

She wonders, *Is it a question?* She can feel his hands tremble, see that his eyes are downcast and lifeless. "But, Hawk, you're the best. You're the best at other things too. You've always been the best."

"I'm not the best anymore, Doreen. I can't deliver three loads a day. I don't have the nerves. I should quit before I make a mistake."

"But what will we...what will you do?"

He turns morose. "I don't know. I don't know anything except driving—just driving. And fishing the river. My parents wanted more for me, expected more of me. When I was a boy I promised them more, promised them I would pursue knowledge and accomplishment. Have I done neither?"

"Charlie, your knowledge is greater than you give yourself credit for. You know more than most college graduates. You're always curious, and you've always read books. You've retained your mother's love of literature."

"But books don't tell me what to do. What's the use of knowledge if it doesn't develop wisdom? Sometimes I think it's wisdom I lack. I don't seem able to convert learning to accomplishment."

She squeezes his hands, compelling him. "Look up at me,

Tamiko. Think about your daughters. Know the enduring love we have for you. Acknowledge what you have done for us, the sacrifices you've made so Michele and Carleen can go to college…an opportunity you and I never had. Isn't that accomplishment?"

"Yes, my family is an accomplishment I'm proud of, maybe the one pride I still have left. But that doesn't seem enough for me." For a moment he stares fiercely at her, then beyond her, and his voice swells to an angry pitch. *"Doreen, I need to do something, something beyond hauling logs."* Then anger leaves him, his eyes again turn passive, and his voice softens as he mumbles, "Doreen, I'm sorry. You're my beloved river creature. I can't…just can't… won't…cause you to suffer too. I'm so sorry."

She removes her hands from his and brushes at tears forming in her eyes. Then, returning her hands to his, she turns them over and gazes at his palms and fingers. "Do something else with your hands, Tamiko. Your fear is in your head, not your hands. You've got good hands. Big hands. Clever hands. Gentle hands. You know how I love your hands on me." She presses his hands to her breasts, squeezing tightly before she finally releases him. "And you're good at woodworking. You could be a carpenter, a really good carpenter."

"But that means the city, Doreen. I'd have to leave the Klamath. I can't do that. How can I leave the Klamath? I've lived here all my life. And my father before me. And his father. No, I can't go to the city. You know that." Sometimes she just didn't understand. He's bonded indelibly to the river by his heritage—three generations of river-dwelling, rural school teachers and countless generations of Hupok Indian chieftains who'd lived on the Klamath for centuries. Bred deeply into Charlie is an abiding love and respect for the river of his ancestors. The Klamath captivated the soul of his youth and has dominated his adult life. Not even fear can overcome his inbred confidence that the Klamath will sustain him.

She steps back, admiring visible signs of her husband's Indian heritage: his light coppery skin, now glistening in starlight like a fine sculpture, and his slate gray eyes...*Is the fierceness gone?*... which, accentuated by high cheekbones, give him a deceivingly stern, hawk-like visage. "Tamiko—Little Hawk," she whispers. "How I love your boyhood name." Then she peers deeper into his eyes, searching. "But, now the raptor's look is gone." She sees only a dull, shadowy lifelessness. "I know the Hawk will never leave the river," she says. "But, Charlie the Hawk, I have a fear too."

"What's that?"

"I can't see temerity in your eyes anymore, only apprehension. Your audacity is gone. It makes me fear the Hawk is becoming a sparrow. And I can't bear to see that happen." She's sometimes derisive when she's impatient with Charlie, and she knows now might not be a good time for derision—but she can't restrain a mocking, "Where has the courage of the Hawk gone? Has the Hawk become a Sparrow?" *Can I shame him into change? Dare I even try? Fail and hate myself after?*

"Don't, Doreen. It doesn't help."

"Charlie the Sparrow? Food for the fishes or food for the hawks?"

"That's enough, Doreen." His face is ashen. "What do you want me to do?"

"I don't know. You have to decide."

They return to the bed and sit side by side, not touching. He buries his face in his hands and speaks slowly. "I should go into the mountains, deep into the Siskiyous and work for the growers."

"No. Please, Charlie." She shrinks from him. "Not the growers!"

"Why not?"

"It's dangerous. You know it's dangerous."

"So...it's dangerous. What I do now is dangerous."

"Working the plantations is too dangerous. And it's dirty work, Charlie. Dirty work for dirty men who run a dirty business."

"Look at Pete and Straw Hat Harry. They're doing okay."

"No, they're not doing okay. They won't tell you. They're too proud to tell you. But they tell their wives. Their wives are terrified. It's the fear of being caught. And it's the fear of getting killed. Bad things happen in the growers' camps. Nobody trusts anybody. The growers are always fighting each other. They import workers to cultivate and harvest their fields. The imports don't like river people. And river people don't like the imports. So they fight. Sometimes river people go into the camps and never come back. You know that. Pete and Straw Hat Harry have been lucky so far, but their wives say their fear is worse than driving fear. If it wasn't for the big money—dirty money is always big—they'd get out. Please, Charlie, don't go to the growers." She turns and holds out her arms, imploring him.

He reaches for her then. "All right, I won't go to the growers, not this time. I'll keep driving. It'll work out. It has to work out." He expresses confidence he doesn't feel.

She shudders in his arms, as feelings of relief she expected don't come to comfort her.

———

BUT IT DIDN'T WORK OUT, did it? Charlie rolled over on his back, stared at the ceiling, and then closed his eyes again. He counted three more trucks and tried to guess how many more until the sun finally rose high enough for its rays to penetrate the Klamath gorge—twelve more maybe. *The sun fights to maintain its presence. It's forced to retreat further south each day.*

Yes, he'd continued to drive, with fear his unwelcome companion. Even now he wondered if that fear might still be inside him, like a seed from a noxious plant lodged somewhere in his mind, just waiting for the right conditions to germinate again. Too well he remembered what that fear was like. It had been a brutal, gut-knotting, irrational, cold, genital-shriveling, uncompromising fear that destroyed his pride. Soon his fear had spawned exhaustion more deadly than fear. And then....

———

HE ENDURES A SLEEPLESS NIGHT after a day off to picnic
with Doreen and fish for steelhead at Wingate Bar. He lies awake,
trying not to disturb her and chastising himself—*Whoever heard
of an Indian forgetting how to sleep?* The next day, he ignores his
morning rush of anxiety and leaves home before daybreak for
the first time in weeks, resolved to make three deliveries. *I must
change*, he thinks. *I can't even enjoy a free day on the river anymore. No stop at Tony Fisheyes tonight*, he vows.

Doreen wakens at the sound of his boots clumping across the
floor. Her first thought: *Why? Why is he putting his boots on inside?*
Her second thought: *He's so heavy-footed now. Even his Indian
stealth has deserted him.* "Oh-h-h, no...no-o-o-o..." she whispers
in agonized words, divining his intent, "he mustn't." Still in her
nightgown, she rushes from their bedroom to intercept him as he
plods through the front door. "Don't, Charlie," she pleads, "please
don't. You're too exhausted; I know you didn't sleep last night."

He turns and hesitates. His lips part slightly, but he remains
silent, shakes his head, and stares at her.

She reaches out and brushes his face with her fingertips.
"Talk to me, Charlie."

His jaw clenches. Again he shakes his head, and he continues
to stare at her. Bathed in faint glow from a setting moon, she's a
haunting vision before him. The vision hints at softness, at sanity,
at safety, and warms a part of his heart he thought fear had chilled
forever. Her eyes hold him captive for a moment, and he watches
her pupils dilate like a frightened animal's. His mind freezes to
his purpose, and he remains devoid of speech.

When she drops her hands to his arm, his visage in moon-
shadow is that of a stranger. She shudders at his appearance, reso-
lute, grim and implacable. "No, Charlie," she gasps, "you don't
have to prove anything." His awful silence stills her voice but not
her tears.

Gently he removes her hands, turns, and strides away.

She stands at the door, sobbing softly into emptiness. *He
didn't say goodbye. First time ever he didn't say goodbye to me.*

EXHAUSTION threatens to collapse his faculties, and he struggles to stay awake. He opens the truck windows and turns up the volume on his radio, but radio waves seldom penetrate the Klamath gorge, and mostly static plays back. *Just forty miles, and I'm in with my third load. I can do that...if I stay focused. How? I know...I'll count creeks. Just passed Wingate Bar...so Clear Creek is next. Think of its tributaries, damn you...you've seen them all. Keep your mind alert. Start at the headwaters. Doe Creek is first...then Preston and Cedar Creek...then West Fork comes in...then Red Hill Creek, no, Bear Pen is before...then Bear Valley and Tenmile Creek...then Fivemile and Slippery Creek...and finally the South Fork which begins as Gum Boot Creek. Okay...I'm making the long swing to the west, so...beyond that promontory, on the other side of the Klamath there's Titus and Tinkham Creek...then Independence Creek...then Ukonom Creek...at least that Indian name survives.*

Ah-h-h...there are too many. My mind can't keep up. I'm forgetting something. But not creeks. Something I forgot this morning. A vision of Doreen in the moonlight occupies his senses. So real... does he only imagine her? She beckons. *Have to hurry...hurry for Doreen. Something I forgot to tell her.* His eyelids flutter and close. *Must tell Doreen. Must tell...what?...can't remember.* He loses concentration and his mind drifts into sleep's precursor, images mostly outside his experience. He's moving fast now, wind whistling in his ears, coasting on his bike down the Paladora. He passes a featureless person who plods uphill on moccasined feet, head bowed as if in prayer. "Go with care, Tamiko," his image speaks to him. "There's something you still must do."

As his head falls forward, his hands slip from the steering wheel. *Charlie's Pride* charges through a curve, jackknifes off the shoulder of Highway 96, and plunges forty feet into the Klamath below. He wakens just before impact, aware first of a rush of air around him, then a powerful blow to the entire left side of his body. A cry, "Aw-w-w no...not now," escapes his lips, and he loses consciousness.

Wakened again, this time by icy water and searing pain, he rises and stands on the submerged left door. His left leg collapses under him, and his left arm dangles uselessly at his side, fingertips touching water; but he remains upright and manages to reach through the right window with his right arm and pull himself free from the sinking truck. A log floats by. He throws his good arm around it and kicks out with his right leg, pushing desperately toward shore. *Dillon Creek is just around the bend. There'll be someone in the campground.* Again he loses consciousness.

SHOCK-BLURRED sensations partially arouse him. Someone yelling at him, pulling at him. *Don't, it hurts...just let me rest... so cold...just let me rest.* Blankets around him and something soft beneath him. Then nothing. Then hazy visions of strange people in white hovering about him, mumbling words he can't hear in voices he doesn't recognize. Finally a voice he hears and recognizes asking "Charlie?"—from someone very close. Then a feeling of fresh tears on his cheek—her tears, not his. With an agony of effort he forces the words he wanted to speak before. "Bye, river creature," he croaks hoarsely, "so...so sorry I forgot."

He feels a cool hand on his forehead, and the voice speaks again. "It's okay, Charlie."

"But...I was afraid...."

"Yes, I know."

"No...not that fear. I was afraid my ancestors' Gods...or yours...wouldn't let me...say goodbye to you."

"No goodbyes, Tamiko. Not now. You're going to be okay."

"Okay? Really? This isn't just...one of my damned visions?"

Then he hears Doreen's familiar, sardonic laugh. "No visions, Hawk. Only reality here. You're in the hospital."

"But there's no pain. Why is there...no pain?"

"Because you've been sedated. You're drugged away from reality, even from your visions. And now you must rest."

He remembers he had an earlier vision, a vision with a voice telling him something else he must do. *But what? Too tired...can't think...can't bring back that vision.* Then he finally sleeps.

CHARLIE and Doreen refuse to call his dunking an accident. "Charlie the Hawk's swan dive," the other drivers call it. "Charlie the Hawk's last swan dive," he calls it. "Charlie the Hawk's first real bath," she calls it.

He misses four months of work recuperating from his injuries: slight concussion, left leg broken in two places, two fractured ribs, broken left elbow, broken collarbone and dislocated shoulder. But he wasn't badly cut. His face was barely scratched. Doreen is thankful he wasn't badly cut. "No more driving," he tells her when he recovers. "The river forgave a mistake. I don't know why. It doesn't do that very often. It likely won't forgive another. I'm through with hauling logs."

Doreen agrees and is relieved. She smiles and hugs him. "You're still the best," she reassures him. She means it.

DOREEN

CHARLIE FINALLY SAT UP and massaged his neck and shoulders. Only a little soreness there. *Good, days off still help.* Instinctively he reached beside him to the empty place on the pillow where Doreen's head once rested. It was a gesture born of habit and the wake-up ritual of ten thousand mornings past. Instead of her cheek, Charlie's hand absently stroked the pillow. *Morning loneliness is the worst. I miss her most in the morning, even more than at night.*

Barefooted he padded over to the half-opened east window and smiled; what he saw pleased him. The sun was just cresting the rock-strewn ridge of Baldy Mountain. Light flooded down its flanks into dense new-growth forests. *New life always replaces the old. Even man can't void the process.* He turned, paced to the still-closed west window, opened it and looked out. *My downriver destiny. Wonder what it will have for me today?*

Maintaining a childhood habit turned adult ritual, he turned his head and closed his eyes. Shutting off his sight permitted him to envision things unseen and enhanced his other senses. He breathed deeply and swelled his lungs to their fullest. The air he inhaled was fresh, clean, cool, and dampened from dissipating river mists. It still carried its morning purity. *No noxious smells from truck exhausts. Not yet.* By late afternoon, the air about his cabin would carry an odor, faint but unmistakable and foul.

Between trucks and through the open window, he liked to greet the river and listen to early sounds from the Klamath gorge.

Good morning river. How are you today? Young and boisterous? Old and grouchy? I know; it depends on my mood. I guess I'm somewhere in between. I know you're mostly ageless. I know where you run swift and bumpy in a cataract...and you make me labor like an oar donkey for safe passage. I know where you're placid and peaceful like a pond...and you allow me a few minutes' rest. I know when you're angry, your voice a raging tempest...and when you're at peace, your voice but a whisper in the wind. He opened his arms and extended them. "Speak to me," he implored.

The Klamath responded, and the brawling rush and babble of nearby rapids greeted him cheerfully. *River sounds, the only constant in my life. My morning tonic. You always soothe me.* In his mind an image formed of turquoise water disappearing into white mists, a river surface glinting in first sunlight like a prism turning. His image brought a companion emotion: hope. A new day's hope to chase away the despairs of yesterday, much as a rising sun dispels the lingering chill of night.

Harsh and angry voices from nearby invaded his reverie, and his hearing adjusted to reality resumed. His neighbors were engaged in their morning ritual: quarreling—with their windows open. Their words were unintelligible, and, as usual, he couldn't identify the subject of their disputes. Nor did he care. He and Doreen had quarreled enough, but never so early in the day. Morning sunlight and disagreement weren't compatible. How could anyone think of anything important to argue about when consciousness was yet an infant?

He opened his eyes and turned away from the window. Rustling sounds, like newspaper pages shuffling, drifted down from his loft and notified him that his resident squirrel family had risen hungry. Then a pair of flickers, who insisted he share his cabin with them too, drummed their first rat-a-tat-tat of the morning on the cabin wall above his head. *Persistent birds. Do they search for bugs or a new nest? Or do they simply make noise to irritate me?* "Careful, my friends," he whispered. "Ancestral urges may overcome me. Not in this century has a Hupok scalped a woodpecker...but don't try my patience."

His mind threatened to drift back again. He wondered if it was a normal thing, this morning preoccupation with his past. Was it part of a traditional aging process? Would he become just another old man telling the same old stories again and again to people who were tired of hearing them, or worse yet reliving past events in a mind that had no space for new thoughts? Or was mind-dwelling in his past merely a natural consequence of living alone? Returning to sit on the bed, he postponed dressing to complete his cycle of remembering. Yes, he would continue to revisit memories, but he vowed to avoid creating images. He should save images for thinking about his future, not waste them on his past.

After he gave up truck driving, he invested the insurance money in college funds for his daughters, a new kitchen for Doreen, and a new drift boat and accessories for himself. Then he signed on with a small timber company as a member of their right-away crew. Occasionally he drove a skidder or a bulldozer, but mostly he grubbed out brush ahead of the fallers and loaded smaller branches left by the buckers. In an ironic role reversal, he became the butt of loggers' scorn. "Hurry up, you Charlie the Pigeon," the loggers yelled at him, "we've got truckers waiting to load and more trees to cut."

Shame pressed against his memory, seeking image recognition. It was good remembering pride, and he didn't mind remembering fear so much. But shame was bad, and he didn't want to remember it anymore. It was a long time ago, and he didn't want to think about his shame. He shook his head to halt memory's advance. *No more images.*

Now he guided fishermen on the Klamath. Five years already rowing a drift boat, and it was the five years before that he wanted to obliterate from memory. Sometimes he missed the feel of a big truck, mostly in early moments of consciousness when he awoke to sounds of engines, gears, brakes, and exhausts, imagined his hands again controlled his destiny and remembered his pride years. But the years of shame he wanted to forget intruded in his thoughts, and then he didn't miss driving anymore. *Enough.*

I need to call Doreen...now. He put his mind to productive work, dressed, and headed for his desk and telephone.

Every Saturday morning he called her before breakfast. She'd moved to Eureka on the coast seven years ago. Sure, he missed her. But he liked to think of her as safe and content. She had a good job working at the city library, good friends, and a small home he'd bought for her. He was relieved she was off the river. "The Klamath gorge is no place for a woman like Doreen," Straw Hat Harry had told him, "not when her children are grown." He knew Harry was right. Charlie and Doreen rarely saw each other now, just occasional weekends. Sometimes he was lonely, but he tried to stay busy and confine his tavern drinking to a solo beer. He looked forward to their Saturday morning conversations. They never ran out of things to say to each other.

She answered after the first ring, and he started their conversation with an animated, "Good news today! I start guiding again tomorrow. A guy from San Francisco. He called last night. Three days he wants. He isn't bringing a partner; wants to fish alone. But he'll pay the full guide fee."

"I'm so glad you're working again, Charlie." She was animated too. Despite their separation, she worried when he didn't work. When he didn't work, she knew he sometimes brooded too much and drank too much, letting shame overtake him. "Did you have any clients last week?"

"No. Not all week, and I'm tired of sitting in a chair reading, tired of work around the cabin, fixing things, building things. It's eight days since I've guided. Fishermen don't request me any more, and outfitters only refer clients to me when they get over-booked on weekends. Then I get the old farts who can't handle themselves or their equipment properly. Either their legs are gone so they can't wade the river anymore, or they're afraid of the river and too ashamed to tell me so they say their legs are gone. Then I have to do all the work with my boat to get them close to a fish, which they never make a decent cast to. Or if they do, they're too slow setting the hook at the strike. Or if they get a hookup, they can't get their fish on the reel fast enough. Or if they do, they've got their drag set too tight and the fish breaks off. And...hell, Doreen, when we don't boat a steelhead, they think I haven't done my job, so there's no tip at the end of the day. And—"

She interrupted him, laughing until she had to cough and clear her throat. "Charlie, excuse me...stop now...stop complaining.... You know you love it. The older fishermen respect your skill and river knowledge. They listen to your advice and don't try to tell you what to do, and they even enjoy listening to your awful Indian stories. They release what they catch without your prompting. They don't keep you on the river so late your arthritis gets bad from the night chill. And they buy you a beer at Tony Fisheyes. You know it's the young fishermen who give you grief. They call you 'Injun Charlie,' and they don't have any respect, for you or for the river. They think they know it all because they've read the right books and watched the right videos. They want to kill everything they catch, and they thrash the river to a froth, frightening everything that swims within a hundred yards. They keep you on the river till dark, go out drinking and whoring all night, and show up the next morning late, hung over, mean, smelly and—"

He was laughing too and interrupted, "Doreen...you stop now. Listen to the two of us...carrying on like all the malcontents at Tony Fisheyes."

"Well, you sure are, with all your complaining about the old farts."

"Me? And what about your gripes about the young studs giving me grief? We both know we're only grouching about the exceptions. Most of my fishermen are decent. If they aren't skilled, they're at least diligent and sincere in their effort. They respect the river, and they respect me a lot, frequently more than I deserve. They're damn good company on the river and mostly generous. Steelhead are the common denominator. Our all-consuming interest in that contrary fish makes us always equal on the river. Do you know what I'm trying to say?"

"Hell, Doreen, I've guided people from all walks of life: a prince, a football hero, a network news anchor who wanted to interview me, an actor/director turned environmentalist who offered me a bit part in a movie, and a former president turned expert fly fisher who hugged me at the end of the day. I've endured a college professor who lectured me...a beautician who wanted to do my long gray hair...loving sweethearts who could barely take their hands off each other long enough to cast and then ignored each other after they caught their first fish...a loveless married couple who didn't say a word to each other and then chattered incessantly after they caught their first fish...a big spender who tipped me with a thousand-dollar check that bounced...a struggling writer who couldn't pay me...a rich heir who wouldn't pay me...a drunk who blessed the fish he caught...a priest who cursed the fish he didn't catch...and a woman tennis star who kissed each fish she caught smack on the lips before I released it. When I guided two literary friends, one was so inspired she put her rod down for an hour to compose a poem; the other asked if she could write a book about the river and me. And—"

Doreen wagged a finger at her phone as she interrupted, "Stop now, Charlie. You've been reading too many novels. You're way exaggerating...and you know it."

"Sure I am...but the point is, when we're together on the river, we're all equal. We're all the same. We all get out of the boat and go to shore when we have to pee. And all we really want to do is catch a steelhead. More than anything. For that time, nothing else matters. Nothing. It's a bond common to all guides and fishermen. We're all hopeless. We're all infected with the same disease. We're all incurable. We're all crazy the very same way."

She was thrilled to hear renewed enthusiasm in his voice. "Charlie, it's so good to hear you excited...and happy. You sound like the old Charlie the Hawk again."

"But I don't know what comes after this booking." His voice turned hesitant and rueful. "The big-city outfitters keep telling me I'm too old and should quit guiding."

"Is that what you want to do, Charlie? Quit?"

"No, I want to stay on the river, even if I can't guide much longer. You know that."

"Then...you're not...not too old." Doreen hoped the hesitancy in her reassurance didn't betray her own uncertainty. *How do I encourage him and still help him face reality?* "You're never too old to do something you still love to do. You can always fish the river for pleasure like you used to, or help train new guides. Dammit Charlie, you're only fifty-six."

"That's old for a guide. Really old. I started when I was fifty-one. You once thought I was too old to guide at forty-six. Most guides come off the river by their forties. Arthritis binds up their shoulders, or they get tired of rising at dawn and rowing until dusk, or they have families and can't live on what a guide can earn, or sometimes they get like truck drivers...their nerves go and fear creeps in. Some just lose their strength. The river isn't difficult if you're strong, but you can't go soft and still row a drift boat all day. Not on the Klamath. Too much fast water. Rapids and standing waves in the chutes are always reaching out to grab you. They'll eat your boat if you don't stay strong. At least I'm still strong enough to row, even if I am the oldest guide on the Klamath."

"And you're still the best, Charlie. You know the Klamath better than any. You were top guide your first three years." She knew how proud Charlie was of those first three years, particularly after so many years of disappointments. "You boated more steelhead than anyone. The other guides all know you're the best." Then she added playfully, "You know how the guides all like to keep score and compete with each other."

"Competition and scoring. That's the game of life, Doreen."

"I don't know why men keep score at everything. You all treat life like a constant competition where achievement is measured only by some kind of score," she teased. "How many goals you make, how many girls you kiss how many times, how many trees you cut, how many loads you deliver, how many logs you sell, how much money you make...or for your ancestors, how many woodpeckers they scalp...how many rooms in your home, how many cars in the driveway, how many beers you drink, how many ducks you shoot—"

"And," he interrupted, "how many sweaters you own, how many hearts you break —"

"And," she quickly retaliated, "how many fish you catch and how big they are, which is always ten percent bigger out of water than in. C'mon, Hawk, you know you can't win this one. Men keep far more scores than women."

He laughed. "I know. You're right. Silly isn't it?"

"Sure it's silly. You all want to do better and don't know how to judge improvement properly. So you keep score. Quality of achievement is too difficult, too subjective to measure, so you concede evaluation to stupid quantitative measurements like counting deaths in war."

"Hey, I surrender! You're the one who brought up the fish count, not me."

"I was trying to encourage you."

"You did; and I thank you. Even without the stupid fish scores, I know I had three incredible years of guiding. I thank the river spirits for those years. They mended a lot of broken dreams." He hesitated, reluctant to let the conversation drift into the difficult time—now almost two years—that followed. More disappointments he didn't like to think about, but they lingered in the fringes of his mind, a residue of discontent.

She sensed the reluctance. "Are you sure you're still strong?" she asked to change the direction of their conversation.

"Yes."

Good, he sounds confident, really confident. "Even on cold, wet days?"

"Mostly. Sometimes my arthritis is too painful for me to row."

"You still know the river?"

"Yes." *Like running down a pilot's checkout. She's check-listing me.* "I know it better than any."

"You know it like a mistress?" She laughed. "It's all right, Charlie. I've always known you love another, a sometimes fickle temptress."

"Yes. The Klamath is like a mistress...like you, maybe. The river comforts me, teases me, surprises me, delights me, teaches

me, scolds me, challenges me, obsesses me, keeps me forever
bound to it."

"It's always the same for you...the river...isn't it?"

He paused and sighed before he answered. "No. Not really.
The river always means the same to me, but it always changes. In
many ways. Every year. And I learn the changes, the new channels, the new hazards, the new holding water, including difficult
lies other guides sometimes avoid. I understand the Klamath, its
seasons and all its moods, and I understand the fish, how they
behave and why. It's knowledge that's imbedded in my being...
from my heritage and from living my entire life on the river.
Youth and energy can never match it."

"How about your nerves...and...the fear?" She continued to
probe gently.

"My nerves are good. And the fear isn't so bad. There's always a little fear, generally before a rough ride through a dangerous chute, but never after. It's a normal apprehension. All guides
experience it. Even the younger ones."

"You're sure fear isn't sneaking up on you like it did when
you were driving?" she persisted. "Particularly at night when
you're alone?"

"Yes, I'm sure."

Doreen could hear strength and confidence in his voice but
remained silent.

After pausing to gather his thoughts, he continued, "And I
think I know why. The river threatens truckers on the highway
above it, because they drive too fast or for too many years. Or
because they push themselves too hard trying to deliver three
loads a day. They tempt fate by denying the exhaustion in their
bodies and in their souls. The Klamath is kinder to those who
boat upon it. Boaters entrust their lives to the Klamath, to the
charity of its moods. But they must respect the river and have
some skill and strength at their oars. They must also have river
savvy and the right instincts. Drift-boat guides have these traits.
Most importantly they don't tempt fate. They aren't foolish like
the truckers. Truckers fight their equipment, the highway and

the river, for they fight time itself. Guides let their craft drift with the river's pace, sometimes placid, sometimes furious. They travel always in a timeless rhythm, a natural harmony that's captive only to currents unconcerned with time."

"And how about shame?" *Careful Doreen, be careful with this subject.* "Have you forgiven yourself, or do you still feel the shame?"

He was silent for a moment. "Sometimes I feel it. When the trucks wake me up and I can't stop imaging the past. Most of the time I can think about the present, what I have to do today, and stop remembering before memory takes me too far."

She was satisfied with his response and the absence of hesitation in his voice. "You're so much a part of the river, Hawk. I know that when I hear you talk about it. And the fishermen must know it too. I don't understand why you aren't working more."

"It's simple. I'm not boating any fish. The damned outfitters have me last on their priority lists. I'm three weeks into the peak of this season, but only six days on the river, and still no adult steelhead. After last year, they say my luck is bad and no one will book me."

"But, how can you boat steelhead if you're not guiding?" *Oh-h-h, I can't believe I said that.* "Aw-w-w, Charlie, I'm sorry, really sorry. What a stupid thing to say."

"It's okay, Doreen. Truth is often painful...to both those who speak and those who hear it." He felt weary for the first time, but then brightened. "I've got three consecutive guiding days ahead of me now. Willie spotted a fresh run in the river just below Happy Camp. I'll put in above and float to Happy Camp tomorrow. I'll be into fresh fish, and my luck is bound to change."

Luck, she fumed. *If it were only so simple.* "Charlie, you've got to think more about the future. Time and the river are running out on you. You can't guide much longer. You know it and I know it. If lack of bookings doesn't end your guiding, your arthritis will. You've got to find something else. I know you're running out of money. What have you done...two trips a week?

And the season only lasts a few months. It's not enough to live on. You can still fish the river for pleasure, but you've got to find some other work."

"My father stayed on the river until he was sixty."

"But he was a commercial fisherman. He was also twice as much Indian as you."

"That didn't make him any stronger."

"No, but it made him twice as stubborn. He stayed ten years too long. When he died a year later, his arthritis was so bad he couldn't dress himself. I don't want that for you, Charlie."

She made him think about things he always put off thinking about. He knew he shouldn't put them off, because it was better to think about the future than the past. Thinking about the future made the past seem unimportant. There was always hope in the future, and hope could be savored, but the past was finality, and finality could only be regretted. The past was over. Done. Unchangeable. "It's okay, Doreen. It'll work out. It has to work out."

It was the same answer he'd given years before, reflecting an evasive ancestral complacency. She remembered and was sad.

He didn't remember and was genuinely hopeful. "I'll call you Tuesday," he promised. "Wish me luck."

She hesitated and finally sighed. "Good luck, Charlie." She tried to sound cheerful.

After disconnecting, she sat quietly for several minutes, studying two photographs framed side by side on her telephone table. She'd placed them where she could see Charlie when she talked to him. One, her favorite, was badly faded. In it her husband stood beside his first truck, one arm around Michele who stood next to him holding his lunch pail in her two small hands. Still an infant, Carleen nestled in his other arm, held tightly to his chest. She looked up at her father, a look of trust and innocence frozen in a timeless moment. Charlie smiled down at Carleen, and his unlined face showed a young man's pride and presumption of invincibility. *My husband as I always want to think of him.*

In the second photograph, he knelt in shallow water beside

his drift boat, the day after Doreen had painted it and helped christen it *Charlie's Pride*. In his hands he cradled a long, silvery fish. Its crimson gill covers expanded as it gasped for breath. Lines of middle-age etched deeply into Charlie's features, and his smile seemed tentative and insecure. He appeared less of the present and more of the future, as he looked neither at his catch nor at the camera, but into the distance, his eyes projecting a haunting sadness. *My husband acknowledging his own mortality?*

Her thoughts continued beyond the second photograph. From it, should she have guessed Charlie's success as a guide would be short lived? In his fourth year of guiding, his catch declined steadily. Despite diminished spawning runs, other guides found ways to keep their catch respectable. Charlie didn't. Then there was the incident. *Yes, the incident.* It still tormented her.

It happened on one of the few autumn weekends she spent with him in their homestead cabin. When she heard his van enter the driveway before noon, she knew something was wrong and rushed to the door. Imprinted forever in her memory was the image then before her.

========

HE STANDS HATLESS and shaking below the doorstep. His clothes are soaking wet, his face ashen, his eyes vacant, lifeless, downcast, and staring. He slumps forward with his legs spread and his knees bent. His arms dangle at his sides as if useless. Neither hand reaches out to the door or to her, and his palms are turned backward. *"Charlie's Pride* is gone," he says simply.

Fear sears into her and she manages a gasping, "Wh…what happened, Charlie?"

His voice is halting and subdued. "Neptune's Whirlpool… uh-h…it got me. I uh-h-h…miscalculated a turn. Broke both oars…on rocks. Jumped free…just before the first swirl sucked the boat in like…like it was a toy…smashed it beyond repair. Nothing left but broken pieces scattered for a mile downriver." He pauses and shuffles his feet as if searching for security from the earth to overcome a loss of sanctuary in his beloved river. "Is this some kind of message…a message from the river…from the Gods of my ancestors? What are they trying to tell me?"

Ignoring his wet clothes, Doreen reaches and draws him close, holds him with all her physical strength, closes her eyes and nestles her head against his shirt, sharing his damp, feeling his body tremble. She wills her energy to infuse him, rescue him. As if providing a mother's warmth and comfort to a child in distress, she strokes the back of his head, neck, and shoulders until she feels his tremors subside. "No hidden messages, Tamiko. You had an accident, just an accident. Are…are you hurt?" She runs her hands over the rest of his body, searching for injury.

"No. Not hurt. And my clients were both strong swimmers." He turns her face up to his, and a small boy's look of surprise and dismay pleads with her for understanding. "The river forgives me again, Doreen. The Klamath forgives me a second mistake. I don't know why."

He mustn't repeat the past, she thinks, as she shudders, gathers her emotional strength, grips his face with both hands, and says, "Charlie, this time you must not quit." With her eyes she pleads for the answer she seeks. She sees color return to his face, fierceness return to his eyes, and she feels his arms encircle her.

"No, not this time," he says as he kisses her. "This time I will not quit."

═══════

AND HE DIDN'T. Doreen looked again at the second photo. *To complete the cycle, we need another photograph. I must remember to take another, before the season is over.* But how would she know when the cycle was complete? *I must wait until his catch improves.* She shook her head, remembering the enigma of season's end the year before.

═══════

AFTER HE FINDS A replacement boat, an older, already river-worn model, she returns to their Klamath cabin to help him christen yet another *Charlie's Pride*. A rush of late bookings makes them both hopeful. Then he endures twenty straight days on the river without a steelhead and ends his guiding season in frustration. His reaction is a mixture of stoicism and confusion. "Another why," he says to her, shaking his head.

In a role reversal, her reaction is a philosophical replica of his usual response to disappointment. She accepts his catch failure as a natural consequence and says, "It's simple, Charlie. Your revered river spirits have declared: 'We gave back your life, but we give you no more of the anadromous trout who are the river's life. Your life for theirs.'"

He nods his head, and she listens patiently to his similar, more allegorical explanation. "It's like an ancient Klamath Indian legend my father passed down to me. As best I could remember, I related it to Straw Hat Harry and Willie McPherson last night at Tony Fisheyes. According to the legend, an Indian boy from the tiny coastal village of Wanakoola was the brightest, most clever, and most successful of all the young Hupok fishermen. His nets were always heavily laden with big, strong and bright, fresh-run fish. Rarely a mark on them, even from harbor seals who shared the harvest with Wanakoola and all the other fishing villages. The tribe believed the boy had a pact with the river spirits, and they marked him early as a future chieftain. One day he fell from his log scaffolding while working his nets. He disappeared and was presumed drowned. Two days later he walked into Wanakoola with no memory of what had happened.

"From that day the boy's nets gathered no fish, and he asked for the lowest tribal task, cleaning fish caught in other nets. But he was cheerful in his work, for he knew the river spirits fairly denied him the river's life in return for granting his life, and he no longer cared to kill any crimson and silver trout from the sea. Despite his menial task, he was still held in high esteem, for the tribe believed he had returned from the dead with great power and wisdom, and with the blessing of the river spirits who had spared his life. In time he was elected chief, fulfilling his destiny. Although the new chief never killed another fish, his tribe prospered and knew no flood, famine, or pestilence during his lifetime."

"What did Harry and Willie say?" she asks.

He hesitates, then frowns and shakes his head. "Aw-w-w, they didn't take me very seriously. 'So-o-o, Charlie,' they teased me, 'you think you'll catch no more steelhead but someday become a tribal chieftain?'"

She knows not to tease him about the Indian legend. She knows there aren't enough generations between Charlie and his primitive Hupok forebears to breed out all the old Indian ways. Tribal superstition can still overcome reasoned logic from the non-Indian side of his mind.

=====

THE IMAGE OF her husband's insecurity portrayed in the second photograph still haunted her. *We no longer talk about the incident or the legend of the young fisherman.* Then she stared at empty table space behind the photographs. *What will the next photograph show? Will there be another?*

SHAME

*T*HE SAME OLD CHARLIE, Doreen mused as she turned away from the photographs. *He remains my half-breed child-husband of two cultures, always part of each, never quite comfortable with either, forever unreconciled with his past. To me he's Tamiko, my Charlie the Hawk, the person I loved yesterday, love today, and will love tomorrow without asking or expecting him to make a commitment to either heritage. But I'm the only one who still uses his boyhood Indian name, the only one since his mother who comes close to understanding his duality and his torments.* She knew she shouldn't push Charlie. It wasn't in his nature to make practical plans for his future. How ironic that she loved him more, not less, for his instinctive reluctance to deal with the realities of his present circumstance.

Once, she'd pushed him too hard, and it was a mistake. She'd pushed him away from his river of salvation *and into those years of shame that still haunt him so.* They were bad memories for her too. But she'd learned to live with them with less regret and more self-forgiveness.

When he quit driving logging trucks, he wanted to guide fishermen on the Klamath. She knew there wouldn't be enough money, so she pushed. "Charlie, we can't live on your guiding income. The season is too short, and there's not much temporary work for you in the off season. I could find work in one of the taverns along the river, but—"

"You know I don't want you working the tavern or tourist trade."

"—but even if I do," she continued, "there won't be enough money for our daughters to finish school. A college education for them is our dream. And theirs. A chance we never had. You won't haul logs, and you won't move to the city, but, dammit, Charlie, you can't start guiding at twice the age of other guides. You've got to find some other work."

KNOWING she was right and stung by her denial, Charlie turned his back on the river and joined a right-away crew working for logging companies. But it was work he couldn't relate to with men whose company he didn't enjoy. Alone in his truck, hauling logs and having a visual or auditory presence of the nearby Klamath for company and comfort, was exhilarating. Being a direct participant with others in destruction of the timbered slopes of his beloved Siskiyous filled him with revulsion. Others took pleasure in dominating nature with their minds, their bodies and their machines. He couldn't. Others reveled in their physical strength. He didn't. Something deep inside him rebelled. Feelings of discontent pursued him. He wondered if those seeds of anger would germinate and flower into something else. He felt trapped in a foreign world not of his choosing from which he was unable to escape.

NOT until later did Doreen hear about his feelings of anger and discontent. But his unhappiness was obvious to her. Feeling powerless to make things better for him, she watched his work slowly eat away at him, like pine beetles gradually destroying a strong, healthy tree. But it was work without fear, until that awful day when their lives changed forever.

CHARLIE was driving a bulldozer, clearing road access for logging trucks into residual stands of old-growth timber, most of them along fringes of sections already logged and showing new growth. Companies willing to accept greater safety risks held the cutting permits. Because the terrain was so rocky and treacherous, the Forest Service had delayed permitting for years—until the easy cuts were finished. Only the toughest crews bid the dangerous work.

Hillsides were soggy and slippery from heavy rains, and he tried to force his machine up a steep slope. Too steep. When the dozer lost traction and began to teeter, he realized his mistake. He cursed and frantically jammed the gears into reverse, but he was too late. The big front blade clipped a large boulder, skidding the machine sideways to the hill. Screaming *"Look out!"* he jumped clear of the dozer's path just before it slipped off an embankment, flipped on its side, and smashed into a crew of choker setters working below. Human limbs splintered like matchsticks. When the heavy machine came to rest, two men were still pinned beneath its roller-track blades.

The twenty minutes it took to free the accident victims seemed an eternity. Their screams of agony burned into his soul, a wound time never healed. Both men were rushed to the hospital, where one died of massive internal injuries. The other lost both legs at the knees. Pensioned off with a new nickname, Tommy Two Stumps remained on the river, spending most of his disability checks in Tony Fisheyes and unintentionally taunting Charlie with a visual reminder of the accident.

The accident investigation was brief, its report short and simple. "Driver error." Two words. Two condemning words that bound him to feelings of guilt and remorse more effectively than prison shackles. The sorrowful eyes of a lonely and resentful widow brought a more compelling accusation and indictment than prosecutor or jury ever could.

Tommy Two Stumps soon found himself enjoying his altered state. A check came in the mail every month, and he didn't have to work for it. He didn't have to worry about his feet freezing in the forest in winter. His family waited on him and spoiled him rotten. Most nights he was the center of attention at Tony Fisheyes. If his disability checks ran dry, there was always someone there to make sure he didn't. He readily forgave Charlie.

But an embittered widow and her three fatherless children never did.

Charlie refused to drive a truck again—any truck. He worked the most menial jobs: loading saws, serving meals, cleaning latrines, filing reports—the only jobs timber companies would give him. Initially he bore his shame with stoicism. Pride was no longer his companion. His pride of heritage retreated into obscurity. His heart pride succumbed to numbness. His mind pride withered and died. He'd destroyed all his prides. "I'm undeserving of pride," he told Doreen with a conviction that defied argument. He brooded with such an intense melancholy that she threatened to throw him out of the house. At least Michele and Carleen were away at school and didn't have to see their father's deterioration.

He gave up boating the river on his days off, which became more and more frequent. The Klamath provided the wine giving his life its natural intoxication. But his wine turned to vinegar. The river's pleasure evaded him. His lifelong love affair with the Klamath was swept away in the swelling tide of a depression he understood but couldn't overcome.

When he finally slept at night, his sleep was fitful and tormented by nightmares. Each night Doreen waited fearfully until he slept and then cried herself to sleep beside him. There seemed no way out of a continuing down-spiral into emotional despair. For either of them.

And then a day she would never forget.

========

SHE HEARS HIM RISE at dawn, dress for the mountains and pack a lunch. He says nothing, and she pretends to be asleep. Apprehension is a growing knot of pain inside her, like menstrual cramps. But she remains silent. He slips out the door, hesitates and glances back, then strides resolutely down the gravel driveway. She races to the window and sees him enter Straw Hat Harry's battered pick-up truck.

THE answer to the question she's afraid to ask shows in his face when he returns late that night. His lips are compressed, his eyes show determination. It's that *stubborn Charlie* look she knows so

well. But there's also something new—a set to his jaw, a shifti-
ness in his eyes, a slight lowering of his head toward his chest. *A
defensive mask I haven't seen before.*

"It's the growers," she wails. It's not a question.

"Yes." His features are impassive.

"You've decided." Still not a question, and tears are in her
eyes now.

"Yes."

"How long?"

"Two years. I've contracted for two years."

"Will you be safe? Oh God, Charlie…will you be safe?"

"I think so." Tears are in his eyes too. Not even his stoicism
can prevent them from welling. The Hawk's eyes are now a wa-
tery dull-gray and lifeless. The raptor's piercing glint is gone. In
its place is the sadness of Hupok ancestors whose blood no longer
flows purely in any descendent. "As long as I don't take chances."

"Oh God, Charlie. Please don't take any chances."

"I won't."

"What work will you do?"

"Carpentry. I'll build their drying sheds, and I'll expand their
camouflage systems. You always say I'm good with my hands."

"I know." She's silent a moment and then speaks softly.
"How will you live?"

"I'll stay in the tent camps. It's safer for both of us if I stay in
the mountains and don't come down."

"Not even on weekends?"

"Not even on weekends. I'll share a tent with Straw Hat
Harry. He's telling Rosie tonight that he's staying in the camps."

"What if you get caught?"

"I won't get caught. Remember I'm half Indian. I know the
mountains as well as the river. No one can catch me there. No
one."

"But…but," she buries her face in her hands, "but…what if
you're killed in the growers' camps?"

"I won't be. I'll do my job. I won't drink. I'll stay away from
the other workers, and I'll stay out of trouble." He pauses and

smiles for the first time, a grim smile. "Hell, I'll be like they say in the western movies—one 'dumb Indian'."

"Dammit Charlie, not the growers!" *Careful Doreen, don't break down now. That won't help.* "You know how I feel about the growers."

"I know. I'm not proud of what I'll be doing."

"Then why, Charlie? Why?" she sobbed. *I have to let it out.*

"I've got to do something. There's nothing for me at the timber companies anymore, not even desk work. They don't want me around. I'm only getting an occasional maintenance or clean-up job when someone feels sorry for me. As long as I'm connected to logging in any way, the accident won't leave my mind. I replay it every day, scolding myself, telling myself what I should have done differently. And it's more than that, something I don't fully understand." He pauses, reaches for her hands and leads her to the window. "Come and look," he says and points to a darkened horizon. There, denuded ridges suggest the one-time presence of a primeval forest in a landscape now barren and reaching in supplication to a starlit sky. "It's what those companies do up there," he continues. "Each year they cut deeper and deeper into our mountains. It's the daily destruction of so many trees who've lived here for centuries. So, what's that to me?" He pauses and rests a hand on her shoulder. "It's as if each tree, like our Klamath blood rocks, contains the soul of one of my ancestors at rest, and cutting the tree severs a Hupok's peaceful eternity. Every night I hear terrible screams, from those I killed or maimed in life and those whose souls I now help wound in death. I have too many remorses, and they're killing me slowly. My guilt hurts you too. I see it in your eyes, and I hear it in your crying when you think I'm asleep. That brings me sorrow worse than shame. I can bear my shame. I can't bear to see you so miserable."

"But...why the growers, Charlie? There must be something else." Her eyes plead with his.

"It's the money, Doreen. They'll pay me ten thousand dollars on the first of every month, in cash. You were right about guiding. There's not enough money in guiding. I know that."

"Screw the money."

He shakes his head. "I can't...I just can't. It's the damned Hupok blood in me. They were the proudest of the Klamath Indians and the most protective of their wealth. Hupoks were obsessed with money, maybe because they lived so far away from sources of their principle wealth, the dentalium shells they collected. They prized those stupid mollusks beyond everything else, even their deerskins and woodpecker scalps. They also believed persistent thinking about money would eventually bring more wealth. I've tried that and it doesn't work. I can't just think about it. I've got to do something."

"But what about the girls? You know we've talked to them about staying away from marijuana and anyone who has anything to do with that dirty business. What do I tell Michele and Carleen?"

"I'll talk to them. I'll tell them the truth. They grew up here. They probably know more about the marijuana plantations than we do. They're away at college now, mostly independent and have their own lives. What I'm doing may not affect them as much as you think. I can't expect them to understand. I'm not sure I understand. But I'll call them...tomorrow before I leave."

"I'll have to leave too, Charlie. I can't stand the thought of living here while you're away in the growers' camps. And...and, goddamit, Charlie, it's such dirty work."

"I know."

"I don't want to be here alone with nothing to do but worry about you."

"I know. Stay three months. I'll have enough money then for a down payment on a home for you in Eureka. You'll be safe there and can find work. You've always been the smartest person in the Klamath gorge. You're sure to find work in the city. I know it's not good for you here anymore. Better for you to be busy in Eureka, make new friends and not think about me so much."

"Charlie, I'm afraid. I'm so afraid."

"I'm afraid too. But fear is better than shame. I can't escape shame here. I've got to get free from it. At least I'll be doing something outside, something in the Siskiyous, something with my hands that isn't destructive of what I see around me. I know that will help. I'll finish the carpentry work in two years. No more. I promise. I'll have plenty of money then, even after college expenses, enough to pay off your mortgage, come back to the river, and guide for a few years."

"Aw...no, Charlie. Not...not the growers." She's close against him now, shaking and sobbing. "It's such dirty work."

"I know." He holds her and strokes her hair, still elegant, long and black, but now streaked with gray.

"Oh, Tamiko. Oh, Charlie the Hawk. I'm sorry. I'm so sorry." She cries for both of them. "You do this for me and for our daughters."

"And also for me," he whispers. Tears well in his eyes and his body trembles.

They cling together for a long time. And there is no more talking, nothing more that can be said. Only her sobs of anguish disturb the silence of the night.

WHY RIVERS?

S UNDAY MORNING'S INVASION of truck noises hadn't bothered him. Saturday conversations with Doreen always left him well-ventilated and feeling better, less susceptible to mind-lingering in his past. *She's the one who brings stability to my life... always.* And, he actually had something to look forward to—three days on the river. He turned his van's rear-view mirror, so he could see his face. Damn, he was actually smiling. Even the lines and wrinkles etched into his face looked less severe. *Maybe the ravages of time and tribulation can be reversed.* Then he laughed at his image and stuck out his tongue. A memory flickered.

Charlie picked up two lunches at Tony Fisheyes and, still chuckling at himself, drove upriver to meet his new client at the River's Edge tackle shop in Happy Camp. If he had to identify with a hometown rather than a river, it would be Happy Camp. Now more than a camp, the small town was Mecca for Klamath River travelers, and it bustled with activity through much of the year. Flowing wild and free for 135 scenic miles to the sea, the river and its recreational resources attracted boating and fishing enthusiasts in their restless search for adventure, as its rich deposits of golden treasure had once enticed miners in their endless search for fortune. Although the Klamath gorge was safe enough for a novice, it also provided challenge and excitement for experts.

When he entered the River's Edge, it was empty except for a lone clerk arranging waders on a rack at the rear of the store.

Charlie waved. "Hi Hawk," the clerk called back. "I just opened up. You're early, way ahead of rush-hour traffic. Guides and fishermen won't be jamming in here for another hour. Gotta impatient client?"

"Yeah. Should be along soon." Charlie stopped at the rod rack. He sorted through the popular models, those designed and built using the most advanced technology: Orvis, Sage, Winston, Powell, and some new Scott rods. At the end of the rack two bamboo rods remained, relics of angling history. Removing one, he held its cork grip in his right hand. With his left hand he caressed the rod with his fingertips. Relishing the touch of a smooth varnished surface and admiring its sheen, he marveled at the builder's skill in creating the rod's hexagonal shaping. Six long, triangular strips of bamboo were tapered, spliced and glued together in three sections, each joined by two ferrules that linked in male-female couplings. A delicate yet powerful functional unit combined symmetry of art, perfection of craft, geometric strength, and a vision of purpose. *Last of a great classic. A Leonard. Priced out of my reach. Most anglers don't look at bamboo any more. Fewer and fewer are built each year. Someday....*

Replacing the rod, he wandered over to the checkout counter. For the...*what?...maybe thousandth time*, he stopped to admire a worn and faded river tribute posted on a wallboard behind the counter. *I don't have to read it. It's forever inscribed in my mind.* Only he knew who'd written it—so many years ago, when they were courting. He closed his eyes and recited from memory.

Why Rivers?
Because, like mountains, they are there.
Because rivers—
Forge bonds of friendship
Unmask pretensions
Punish rascals
Restore courage
Inspire poets
Bring humility to the proud and pride to the humble

Encourage harmony and discourage discord
Capture imaginations and free minds from worldly cares.
And because rivers—
Conceal secrets but reveal virtues
Confine sadness to yesterday and liberate for tomorrow the
  joy imprisoned in sorrowful hearts
Replace artificiality with reality
Destroy cynicism but create optimism
Confront fears and build self-confidence
Reward simple achievements with the unabashed and
  boundless feelings of exultation inspired by every
  triumph—no matter if its size be small.
There's an urgency to a river that lets you know it has a date
  with the sea.

For their dates with adventure, white-water thrill-seekers braved the Klamath's cataracts in springtime. Seeking a less hazardous experience, river rafters and canoers flocked to the river in summer, filling its campgrounds. In most years, fishermen congregated when the river cooled and grew more complacent. River lodges filled with those enticed by the Klamath fishery. Many were affluent sportsmen who could afford to have a guide show them the way of the river and its anadromous fish. Many fishermen still killed their catch, sometimes for food, but mostly for vanity. A kill satisfied their need to display a testament to skill and success. Some needed to capture a trophy for vacant wall space and, through a lifeless mount, consign proof of their prowess to perpetuity. Each year more and more anglers fished neither for food, vanity, nor trophy. They came for the thrill of the hunt, and they released their catch without resentment or nagging reluctance.

Charlie hoped his new client wasn't a killer. Like the Hupok boy of the Indian legend, he no longer enjoyed harvesting river life. Guides knew that their livelihoods depended on a living river. Most acknowledged that runs of anadromous fish were declining, erratic, and unpredictable. Some years, fish were plentiful and the river taunted the guides with a false promise of prosperity's return. Most years, fish were scarce and the river confronted the guides with the reality of a resource slowly dying. In the easy, early years steelhead and salmon runs had surged into the Klamath—wave after wave of flashing silvery bodies that seemed never to end. A continuous tide of life had pulsed into the river from a generous sea whose fertility defied exhaustion. Then came the white man, and the ultimate predator plundered the river's bounty. Now the years turned hard and lean, and a new generation of guides and fishermen suffered the river's reprisals.

Too many decades of over-harvesting, both commercial and sport, had depleted the fishery, perhaps beyond restoration. Hatchery programs helped revive steelhead runs, at least in part. "Government pets," some guides contemptuously called the stocked fish. Wild strains of native trout were most prized, for their brilliance of color, their stamina, and their fighting qualities. Few remained in the river. Any guide who encouraged his fishermen to kill their catch foolishly eliminated spawning units and jeopardized his future. Most guides, even those with Indian heritage that bred an instinct for killing for food, now urged their clients to return their catch.

But I can't greet a new client with a question about his kill preference, Charlie thought, as he turned from the counter and appraised a fisherman approaching him. *Must be my client…right on time.* Generally, he could sense a killer. But he couldn't tell yet about the man before him.

Sometimes you could learn a lot about a man from his clothes, from the way he moved, and from his face, particularly if he looked at you directly or avoided eye contact; and not so much from what he said, but from the inflection and tone to his voice when he spoke. Most of the time you had to wait until you were on the river. The river would reveal the character of the man. It always did.

Charlie's appraisal was quick but extensive. *Wearing the right clothes, not too expensive but clothes I'll never have money enough to buy. Colors not too bright…that's good. A pale blue, zip turtle-*

neck, probably one of those artificial fibers that don't keep your body stewing in its own sweat...gray rag wool sweater with leather patch elbows...gray cords and those lightweight combination leather and Gore-Tex walking shoes, probably classic L.L.Bean. Clothes fit like they were tailored. Wears them with flair and a touch of vanity. Everything looks brand new. So he's a novice? If so, he's done his homework or had some good coaching on what to wear. When I see his tackle, I'll know if he's a novice. I'll have to see his tackle to be sure.

Oh-oh, I hope he's not one of those loud and obnoxious party-boat fishermen who expects me to be both servant and guide.

No suntan. So not an outdoor type. The poor fellow has the pallor of an urban cliff dweller...a victim of San Francisco's fogs and vapors. Still young though...about thirty I'd guess. Average height and build. He looks quick and strong. Probably an athletic club junkie addicted to indoor exercise and tasteless health foods.

He has indoor hands. No calluses or broken fingernails, so must be office hands...strangers to outdoor work. But there is power there...power and grace. He'll need both to fish for steelhead.

Blue eyes...bold and aggressive. Compelling, no-nonsense eyes. Is there ruthlessness there? Contempt? Has he forsaken compassion for ambition? I wonder why. Expressionless features...the kinds that rarely display emotion. Has he been disciplined to mask his feelings? Or is that just a city dweller's protective cover?

Thin lips. I don't like thin lips. Is there cruelty there? Or just grimness? Why do I see cruelty in thin lips? A killer's lips?

I wonder of he's a killer. I can't sense if he is. Goddam, I'm becoming one critical guide. So what if he is a killer? As long as he has a license and pays my fee, he's entitled to take a fish. But I hope he isn't a killer.

The inspection was mutual. The fisherman's visual appraisal of his guide was somewhat contemptuous and more experienced, but no more thorough or candid. *Faded levis, no belt...checked brown and gray flannel shirt, clean but washed threadbare, with one button missing...ancient boots with bald treads and broken laces with the loose ends knotted. Generic river wear for a generic river guide who can't afford new clothes.*

Look at that hat. Here's a guide with a sense of humor…a self-deprecating sense of humor? He's not afraid to sport outlandish headgear. It's a rakish, almost affected hat, except it's so dilapidated, dirty and sweat-stained. No self-respecting Californian would wear anything like that, even on a river where nobody important would see it. Big black cone-shaped thing…looks like a miniature tepee. Even when it was new, it was an ugly hat. Oh, no, it's even got a feather in the band.

He's tall, but stooped and a little paunchy. Well into middle age. Too much booze and bad food, and too little of the right kind of exercise. Shows other signs of aging. Moves slowly. Decided limp in his left leg, and he seems to favor his left arm. Some old injuries there. Still strong though. Look at his arms and shoulders. More upper-body strength than some of the guys who work weights at the club. I guess a river guide needs more brawn than brains. Interesting hands…sensitive but obviously powerful. A lot of miles on those hands…look like they've settled a few arguments. I don't think I want to argue with those hands.

Gray eyes…that bore straight into you. I see why he's called the Hawk. A lot of pain in those eyes. Some anger too. The Hawk is not content. They say he's half Hupok Indian. The anguish of a dying race is in those eyes. But there's more there…wonder if he'll tell me. Still clear too. So maybe he's not a drinker. Is there intelligence in those eyes? I'll need to be careful. Charlie the Hawk may be a lot more than a journeyman river guide.

Signs of stubbornness in his features…the way his jaw shelves forward. But no indication of guile. That's good…I don't want to deal with guile from a damn Indian. Stubbornness I can handle. Not guile. He has smiler's wrinkles about his mouth. Laughter's telltale signs…from happier times?

They said he's one of the best guides on the river. He looks it. I wonder, though. How was I able to book him on such short notice? Something wrong? Or did he have a cancellation? I'll have to find out why he was so available, decide if I can trust him. I can't risk using a guide who drinks too much or has lost his strength…or his nerve.

The fisherman was first to break their silence. "You must be Charlie. The Hawk, they told me. I saw your boat outside. I'm Alden, Alden Morse from San Francisco."

"Hello, Alden. Welcome to the Klamath. Yeah, they call me the Hawk."

Their handshake was firm, sincere, but inquisitive. Their eyes held. Not friendly, but not hostile. Not aggressive, but not submissive. Just impassively neutral, as if each held back something he didn't want the other to sense.

"How was the drive?" Charlie asked.

"The drive was fine," Alden responded. "Longer than I expected. The highway was all curves. Tricky at night. I knew the river was below, but I only glimpsed it occasionally when the gorge opened up."

"Sometimes tricky during the day, too. I'll have to tell you some stories about those curves." Charlie's smile was enigmatic. "Before we leave for the river, I'll need to see your license...and your tackle, to make sure you have what you need."

Outside, they unloaded Alden's equipment from the rear of a rental car, an all-wheel-drive foreign model. *Can't tell much about him from the car*, Charlie thought. "Looks like you have a proper rod there," he said. "Nine foot for a six-weight line." He removed the rod from its tube and examined it.

"Big enough?" Alden asked.

"Should be. Klamath steelhead don't run huge. Not as big as fish in the Eel River or the coastal rivers of Oregon and Washington. But they run strong. That's why they're so prized. A six-weight will let you know you've got some work to do to boat a Klamath fish. But you won't be overpowered. By the way, you need to take better care of that rod; your line guides are encrusted with dirt. Now let's see your reel."

Alden handed him a leather reel pouch.

Charlie opened it and smiled. "Wow, an old Hardy Princess," he said. *A rendezvous with history*, he thought. "Newer reels have more advanced technology, but for decades there was no reel finer than a Hardy Princess." He handled the classic reel with reverence as he tested its drag. "When you have a fish on, this reel still talks to you better than any. Hell, it doesn't talk, it screams." Stripping nine feet of leader from the reel, he listened to its ratcheting response with a smile of approval. He confirmed that the leader was tightly secured by a blood knot to a three-foot butt section spliced into the end of the fly line with an improved nail knot. *Looks like a tackle shop tie.* "What leader do you have here?"

"A steelhead taper, nine feet to 3X, I think."

"Is it new? An old leader can go bad on you and cost you a fish."

"Brand new. Is it strong enough?"

"The 3X gives you an eight-pound test tippet. That should be strong enough. Let me check it." Charlie started with the butt end of the leader and carefully stretched it in his hands, a three-foot section at a time, feeling for any flaws or other weakness. "Feels okay." Then he looked closely at the first few feet of the fly line. "Weight-forward floating line. That's good. Now, let's have a look at your waders."

From his gear bag, Alden extracted murky-brown, chest-high waders, grime-encrusted and showing multiple patches, boot-feet clogged with dirt.

Charlie frowned. "You need to keep these clean and stored out of sunlight, or they'll rot out on you. Later in the season you'd need warmer neoprenes, but these should be okay now. They're an interesting brand. Bulletproof waders they call them."

"Why bulletproof?"

Charlie shrugged his shoulders and chuckled. "Dunno," he said. "They're not much protection if someone's shooting at you."

"I'll try to remember to duck," Alden said. "Do you need to see my flies? I've got mostly classic patterns: the Skunk, Skykomish Sunrise, Silver Hilton, and others whose names I can't begin to remember."

Charlie scanned Alden's fly box. "You've got a good selection here, and I tied several dozen flies last week. Between us we've got enough flies to outfit the entire fleet. Now let's wader up and load the boat."

Gouged, scarred, and stained—but clean, Charlie's drift boat rested on the trailer behind his van. He patted the transom, where *Charlie's Pride* was lettered in black script on a vermillion plaque. "My boat's the traditional McKenzie River style," he said. "Best design ever...for any river anywhere."

Alden nodded.

After transferring his client's gear, Charlie opened a battered cooler behind the guide's seat in the middle of his boat and took inventory. All there. Styrofoam containers protected lunch: fresh ham and cheese sandwiches three inches thick on sourdough bread, doused with mayonnaise and slabbed with a red onion slice; macaroni salad, potato chips, two apples, and two huge slices of fresh-baked chocolate cake, all put up at five-thirty A.M. by the breakfast chef at Tony Fisheyes. Calories burned fast on the Klamath. A dozen drift boats were booked for the day; all would enjoy the same high-calorie fare. A six-pack of Coca-Cola and a six-pack of Olympia Beer nestled against a fresh block of ice, together with a gallon water jug.

Then he checked the dry storage area under the stern, containing sweaters, rain jackets, and extra clothing—also life vests in case of a dunking. He showed the vests to Alden. *Gotta be sure he knows where they are,* Charlie thought. "Only needed them once," he said but didn't elaborate.

Alden absorbed, nodded, and remained silent.

For a moment Charlie stared vacantly downriver and felt his body begin to tremble. *Another damned flashback.*

———

FEELING HELPLESS HE SITS stunned, staring in disbelief at two splintered oars as Neptune's Whirlpool sucks him under and gobbles up his boat. When the vortex spits back its captain and passengers, the three flounder in the tumult. But the water isn't deep, and they finally crawl to shore a hundred yards downstream. Then he's lying face down with the river still lapping at his feet, his fingers extended and digging deeper and deeper into the sand, trying to anchor his body safely to land. Wet and exhausted, chest heaving, heart threatening to burst, feeling lost, and shaking from the cold, he lies there coughing and spitting water, tasting near-tragedy's sour residue of fear.

———

YES, HE HAD NEEDED life vests that day, but there had been no time to reach for them. Like most river accidents, the incident had developed too quickly. To clear his mind, Charlie shook his head.

"Shouldn't we wear the vests?" Alden asked.

"Can if you want." His trembling over, Charlie laughed. His client was indeed a novice, at least to drift boats. "Most don't. Vests interfere with freedom of movement you need to cast, and they really get in your way when you're trying to manage an angry fish at the end of your line. Boating regulations require we carry them despite their false security, and they're always there if we need them." *But always just beyond reach. A well-intentioned but ineffective safety precaution.* Charlie didn't mention the incident. *No point in alarming him. Neptune won't get me a second time.*

As Charlie backed his boat down, morning fog misted off the Klamath like escaping night wraiths chased from their river sanctuary. Autumn brought a slight chill to the morning air. Only hilltops acknowledged sunrise. In its more sheltered canyon stretches, gilding of the river was still hours away. The Klamath flowed strong and impassive, dark and unrevealing. In a few months, swelled to full spate by winter rains and high country snows, the Klamath would rage against its banks, wild and untamed for another hundred miles to the sea. Now the river was low and docile, and Charlie's van and trailer jostled and bumped over fifty feet of exposed river bottom, as if cautiously exploring a new cobblestone street. Here the Klamath burbled along over multi-colored, water-smoothed stones: white marble streaked in gray, silver granite, occasional blue schist, black pillow basalt, even blacker peridotite, and other ancient boulders from the Klamath gorge. The river mixed rocks from all eras, as if the hodgepodge geologic pot of the Klamath was stirred into a well-ordered geometric pattern by a master artisan. *Wara arranges his play marbles into friendly welcome signs for us,* Charlie thought, as he surveyed the river bottom in front of him.

When he wrestled his boat free from its trailer, it slipped easily into placid waters, riding high. Specifically designed for big rivers of the Pacific Northwest, the McKenzie boat displaced a minimal draft even when fully loaded. Its high, curved stern knifed safely through the most dangerous troughs and cataracts. Its shallow draft enabled the McKenzie to slide untouched through rapids and over the Klamath's treacherous serpentine boulders, blood rocks whose tops, like ocean reefs, often washed just under the surface, menacing all river traffic.

"Two boats are ahead of us," Charlie announced, gazing downriver.

Alden looked too but saw nothing. *Either the Hawk has telescopic vision or he sees tracks on shore I can't read,* he thought. "How can you tell?" he said.

Charlie laughed. "We passed their trucks and empty trailers back in the parking area. I was looking to see how far ahead they might be. One boat belongs to Wandering Willie, that's Willie McPherson. He's one of our more colorful guides. Loves to sing Scottish ballads on the river and likes to launch before sunrise. I didn't recognize the other truck."

"So we're not first on the river. Isn't that a problem?" Alden's question was confrontive, suggesting an accusation.

"No, not unless it's a problem for you. There's plenty of room here. Some think it's important to be first on the river. They're the impatient ones. Willie's an exception. Being first on the river isn't important to him. Seeing first sunlight from his boat is. That's his inspiration. Occasionally first boats get you into a fish you'd otherwise miss, but other things are lots more important."

"Such as?" Alden was still confrontational.

"How well a guide knows the river and its fish and how well he handles his boat. How well a fisherman can cast, how well he can wade, what fly he selects, and how well and where he presents it." Charlie's tone was challenging. "And that's only to the point of strike. Then there's—"

"Okay, Hawk, I get the message," Alden interrupted. "Just do your part. I'll handle mine."

"And I'll do the best I can for you." Charlie was developing a strong dislike for this man. It was hard not to like a fisherman, particularly a novice. But it happened sometimes. And it made Charlie feel frustrated and angry at himself. "But there's more to it than either of us can control."

"So, what else is so important?" Alden was resigned to hearing the rest of the lesson, despite his lack of enthusiasm for becoming that well informed.

"All the factors neither of us can influence: weather, condition of the water, mood of the fish, and even, although there are a lot of arguments about this, the phase of the moon. We can't do anything about those. The most important factor may be fortune's caprice, being in the right place at the right time. In other words, just plain luck. Some have it, most don't."

"That's not very encouraging." Alden frowned. *A litany of excuses in case we don't catch anything*, he thought. "I've caught a few trout," he said. "Hell, a steelhead is just a small trout who goes to the ocean, becomes a glutton, and stuffs himself on the bounty of the sea until he grows into a bigger trout. I didn't think catching one would be that difficult."

"Steelhead aren't that difficult. They're more difficult. And I'm not trying to set you up for failure. You're obviously new at this, and I'm just trying to be realistic. Steelhead fishing isn't easy. Not on this river. It's very, very tough. It reverts expert trout fishermen to frustrated beginners. Fishing the Klamath can drive a professional athlete to physical and mental exhaustion. It reduces the most articulate genius to a babbling idiot. But when you finally catch a steelhead, and many do because they persist and accept disappointment as a natural part of the chase, the

thrill of the moment will make all your agonies bearable. And..."
Charlie stopped abruptly and smiled. "End of first-day lecture.
I'm really sorry. I'll do the best I can to get you into a decent fish.
Let's go catch a steelhead."

Both had donned waders while talking. What Charlie saved
by cycling his river clothing beyond a normal service life he invested in his waders. "I have to live in these damn things nearly
every day of the season," he'd told Doreen. "And I need to stay
dry and warm when the rains come. I'll get the best. But I can
only afford one pair. That means I'll have to sweat like a logger
in heat early in the season to avoid getting chilled later." His
stocking-foot waders were dark blue neoprene three millimeters
thick, four millimeters in the foot, specially made for river guides.
On cold days, he wore a fleeced Capilene body suit under his
waders for extra warmth. The manufacturer boasted an olfactory
advantage over their competition: an artificial fabric that wicked
away both moisture and unpleasant odors. Doreen had disputed
this claim. "Used underwear is used underwear," she'd said. "It
always smells of stale beer, fish, sweat, and farts, no matter how
much you pay for it or how well you wash it. I know because I
still help you with laundry...occasionally."

For an overboot, Charlie chose a molded plastic model, cus-
tom designed by an Italian ski boot manufacturer. It provided
more comfort and more protection than any of the cheaper models. Its sturdy construction kept it in service through several bi-
ennial cycles of felt-bottom replacement. Eleven machine screws
embedded in each felt sole improved purchase on slime-covered
rocks.

While Alden finished rigging his rod, Charlie drove back to
the parking area. When he returned, he added a final touch to
his preparations for launch. At the bow of his boat, he unfurled a
small flag affixed to a flexible staff which could be folded snugly
along the gunnels so it wouldn't interfere with casting. Hand
sewn and finely stitched by Doreen, the flag was bisected by a
blue slash diagonally and displayed a silver and gray hawk's head
on one side and a red-striped, arcing fish on the other.

"Where do you want me?" asked Alden, wading out to the boat.

"Take the stern seat," Charlie instructed. His client made the same mistake most fishermen did and veered to the bow. Charlie laughed. "Wrong end, Alden. The high end is actually the stern and the bow is lower. As in all rowed boats, I sit facing the stern. The boat is designed so you can stand and cast from there. Those cleats along the edge at top are for you to wedge into and stabilize your footing. We drift stern first so I can see downriver.

"First day with a new client, I like to put in here above Long Riffle," Charlie explained as they glided into the current. "We'll beach on the other side, get out, and wade-fish from the riffle's shallower inner curve. This run often holds a lot of fish. It's also the best place on the river for you to develop technique and for me to evaluate how well you cast."

"I spent an evening last week looking at videos," Alden said, a smug expression on his face. "I think I understand the casting technique. It's logical and doesn't look complicated."

"Ah, yes," Charlie sputtered. "Better preparation for better fishing through modern technology. Videos. They stuff your head with a bunch of nonsense you don't need to know and won't ever use. Then, when you're on the river, you can't remember what you need to know and spend all your time trying to duplicate what you think you saw the guy on the tape do and end up angry and frustrated when you find out you can't."

"It's no different from you showing me, is it?" Alden needled.

"Not much, I suppose," Charlie fumed. "Damn videos are going to take the guides out of guiding. Soon fishermen won't need a guide, just a portable TV and an oar donkey. Maybe someday, someone will even invent a lightweight, hand-held instructional device...whoops...and maybe something better than an aging guide with a faulty mind. Sorry, Alden, we've got to turn around. Hang on." Charlie juggled his oars into a spinning maneuver, reversed his boat's direction, and headed back to shore.

"What the...?" Alden sputtered.

"Car keys. I forgot to wedge them in behind the front bumper for the shuttle service. Later this morning, the River's Edge will transfer the van and trailer to our takeout ramp. Otherwise... let's say we're in trouble." Grounding the boat, Charlie winced and leaped out. "Be right back," he growled. Then he stumbled on up the river bank, shaking his head and muttering to himself.

A forgetful guide? Alden wondered. *That's not a good start.*

THE DRAGON'S TOOTH

"*COVERING THE WATER* it's called," Charlie explained as he waded nearly waist-deep in Long Riffle with Alden beside him. The river's surge applied constant pressure against his legs and hips, but his boots held firm. He kept his body sideways to the current and leaned slightly into the flow, feeling comfortable at this wading depth. At shallower depths, with surface pressure against his knees or thighs, he felt unsteady. He knew he was losing leg strength and balance. His legs trembled when he waded too long in heavy, shallow currents. With half his weight or more beneath the surface, he regained balance confidence. Then the river's current felt like a genial and supportive traveling companion, rather than a treacherous adversary always testing his legs. "The aging process is inevitable," Doreen had reminded him, when, in his third year of guiding, he complained of breathlessness and increasing episodes of embarrassing spills wading at knee depth. "Your lungs and legs are river-worn and age-weary. You can't wade-dominate the river forever." Doreen was right, and he became a more prudent wader. But he hated moving with old man's caution, as he called it. He envied the other guides who still charge-waded the river with unconcerned abandonment and the presumed invincibility of youth.

"The casting technique isn't difficult if you can throw a long line," Charlie began his instruction. "However, drifting an artificial fly is difficult. Everyone has trouble with mending the line so the fly drifts properly. If you don't mend, the fly's natural drift with the current is interrupted because the line moves faster than the fly. It's called drag, and it's a steelheader's curse. The fish recognize something is wrong, sense the deception, and they won't strike. The trick is to keep your line straight by repeatedly mending it." He demonstrated with a short forty-foot cast quartering upstream. Then with a long, graceful sweep of his arm and shoulder, and in a single fluid motion, he lifted the line from the water and let it settle again a few yards upstream. The drift remained drag-free and true for only a few seconds before the current began to belly the line downstream and below the leader. Several repetitions of the mending maneuver permitted the fly to continue its swing in a long, drag-free curve, completing its drift directly downstream of Alden. Barely visible in the water, an artificial creature fluttered in imitation of a delicate living thing suspended beneath the surface and struggling provocatively against the current. "See how the fly stays ahead of the line?"

Alden feigned patience and nodded.

Charlie continued the process, each time lengthening his cast by a few feet. Soon the entire fly line, nearly a hundred feet, extended from reel through rod tip to leader butt. Then he stripped half the line in, coiling it in his mouth to keep it from tangling on the surface, moved five steps downstream, and cast again.

Alden watched closely as Charlie executed a peculiar movement. Just as he lifted the line from the water, his left hand reached to the rod's first guide and stripped in three feet of line in a sudden, jerking motion. As the line curved in a geometrically perfect, elliptical arc behind him, he let the force of his back-cast return his hand to the first guide where it paused a second before repeating the jerky, stripping maneuver as he power cast forward. *Wow,* Alden thought, *all the line shoots back out with only one false cast forward. Gotta be the double haul, like that guy in the video. Looks tricky.*

"Once your line is out, you cover the entire riffle by continuing to move downstream after each cast," Charlie said.

Again Alden nodded impassively.

Charlie continued his instruction. "In a riffle like this, of uniform depth and moderate, constant speed, the steelhead hold anywhere there is a slight underwater obstacle interrupting the current. In other runs there are only a few predictable lies, and we only fish those. Here a fish could be anywhere, and we methodically present the fly to all the water we can. The technique is tedious and tiring with so much line out, but it can be productive if the mood of the fish is right. Here, you try." He passed the rod to Alden. "First with only thirty or forty feet of line…until you get the hang of it."

With an expert's eye, Charlie evaluated his client. He knew that the better trout fishermen generally displayed a high skill level, even if they were inexperienced with heavier tackle needed for steelhead. Years of trout fishing made an angler's technique instinctive, like driving cars, and, with some help from a guide, readily transferable to larger quarry. Alden was not one of the better trout fishermen.

"Keep your rod higher when you back-cast," Charlie instructed. "Stiffen your wrist, move your hand around so your thumb's on top, try to raise your upper arm above your shoulder on the back-cast, and stop at two o'clock. Then pause for an extra second before you power cast forward." Alden's casting technique was worse than inadequate. *No way he can handle a long cast,* Charlie groaned to himself. "Do you know the double haul?"

"No. I saw you do it and watched it on tape, but I'm afraid I didn't practice it. Guess I should have prepared better…more than just watching videos."

"Yeah, that might have helped." Charlie grimaced. *But I doubt it,* he thought.

"So, what do you suggest?"

"We'll stay here in Long Riffle for a while. See if we can improve your casting. If not, we can fish most of the lies downriver from the boat. All you do is hold the rod. I position the boat and back-row to give you a slow drift over the lie." *Damn, I'll have to do all the work for this one today. And my shoulders will throb all night.*

Long Riffle kept them occupied through mid-morning. Mountains protecting the Klamath gorge to the east finally relinquished their control of the horizon. As if cast by a magical golden wand, rays of light seared into the river and unlocked its mysteries. Shadows disappeared. Murky depths became crystalline flashes of interlocking underwater structures. A complete subsurface countryside extended as far as the Polaroid-assisted eye could see. Hills of burnished stone emerged from nugget-strewn valleys. Sandy roadways connected sprawling villages where cottages of gilded rock and rubble glistened with their morning coat of fresh sunshine.

Alden finished working the riffle in flattened glides of its tailing waters. Here the river widened before it narrowed, gathered strength, bullied its way through a funneling, narrow flume, and then, in a burst of foam and fury, boiled into a long, deep pool below. There the river paused in its mad dash to the sea, rested, and renewed its energy for the repetition to follow.

Charlie's mind strayed to his father's mythical description of the river. *Angry water...then placid water...then angry water again.* A thousand times he'd seen the turbulence-to-calm dichotomy replicate itself, again and again, mile after mile, as the Klamath carved its way through the northern California mountains. He closed his eyes to help capture another thought. *Yes, Doreen, it is indeed on its way to keep a date with the sea.* Then he mused further on his river's complete sequence of life. *Wherever high mountains gather water from the storms of winter, wild rivers are born. And a wild river's repetitive contradictions—fury and peace—are forever its personality, forever its conflict, forever its allure. This river was created doubly so because it was twice born...first birthed in the snowcapped Cascades, then rescued from threatened extinction in a volcanic desert plateau and rebirthed in the ancient rocks of our Klamath mountain ranges. So the river we see here is a teenager. It alternates from an awkward and rowdy boy to a graceful and serene young ballerina. After learning from the land, both find maturity and mate in the wisdom of the sea.*

He broke his reverie, opened his eyes, shaded them with a hand, and gazed into the calm water just beyond his client. It was uncanny how fish could hold undetected in the most visible lies, even to the most trained eye. He knew this, but he searched the water anyway, hoping for some telltale flash of movement or color. Sometimes he could see a big fish holding in shallow tailing water just above the long ridge that marked a sudden change in river velocity. Steelhead often rested there, after the exertion of fighting through heavier currents below. He squinted and scanned the ridge line again. No flashes of motion or color. *Nothing there. I'm not surprised. Alden disturbed the whole run with his sloppy casting. He's not a serious fisherman. Less than three hours into the day, and I can tell.*

He knew serious fishermen were all alike. They came for the lure of the hunt, the thrill of a strike, the exhilaration of the fight using light tackle, and the sense of satisfaction that came, not by killing a fish, but by seeing a wild fish lying spent in the shallows, gill plates heaving, waiting to be released. All serious fishermen had a recognizable presence on the river. He could tell by the way they positioned themselves—crouched forward—and by the way their eyes fixed on the point where the line sank beneath the surface, a concentration so fierce it could be broken only by exhaustion or nightfall. *This boy doesn't have it. He's an indifferent caster, despite all the energy he squanders in the effort. Two hours in Long Riffle, and he still struggles to throw forty or fifty feet of line... with no prospect for improvement.*

Backing a few feet to the side and behind Alden, Charlie shook his head in disgust and growled, "You're still buggy-whipping it. Too much wrist and too much elbow. Not enough arm and shoulder. Let your rod and line do the work. Quit babying your rod. Make your rod shoot the line. It can take more stress than you think."

The rapid fire instruction was too much for Alden. "Slow down, dammit...I'm trying," he growled back.

"You're not picking enough line off the water on the mend. You're too jerky. Sweep it. Relax and sweep it. Start lower, end higher. Like this." Charlie stepped into Alden's view and again demonstrated the motion with an exaggerated sweep of his arm.

In resentment, Alden ignored Charlie's advice and flailed at the river, as a petulant schoolboy might react to an unwelcome lecture. "There, is that better?" his voice a model of mockery.

"Not really." Charlie was grim and merciless. "Your rod is still too low in the back-cast, and you're not pausing long enough. Your line loop is too wide and needs to be tighter. And you're making way too many false casts."

"Well, goddamit. Who gives a shit? As long as I put it out there. The fish aren't going to critique me before they decide to strike." In anger Alden executed a final false cast and powered the rod forward. Line and leader uncurled and fully extended in midair. The fly executed a graceful turnover and settled on the water with a gentle splat, one of Alden's better casts.

Unseen and unheard by Alden, Charlie nodded his head and chuckled in approval, but he couldn't resist continuing the heckle. "It's all that extra effort, boy. You'll wear out before noon." Charlie could see a red flush rising in his client's neck and cheeks. *The boy has a bad temper. And no patience.*

"Look, pops, I'll worry about the effort. You take care of the boat. And don't, goddamit, call me boy." Alden's face was crimson. "Just put me where the fish are and I'll catch one."

"I'm sorry," Charlie apologized. "Maybe I was being too rough. Sometimes I get frustrated having to nursemaid beginners down this river. So many come expecting it to be easy. It isn't easy. And when they find out it isn't easy, they expect me somehow to make it easy. And I can't."

"Well, isn't that your job?" Alden was feeling better and more confident, now that he had his guide on the defensive. "How the hell else does a beginner learn, if a guide doesn't show him?"

"It's not my job to teach. It is my job to find the fish, if they're in the river, position the boat, and give you some idea of the right equipment and fly to use. And…oh yes, I make sure you get fed enough at lunch and have cold beer in the cooler. I even provide toilet paper. But I can't cast for you, and I can't mend for you. If you can't do those properly, you might as well stay home, watch videos, and read outdoor magazines."

"So, how the hell do I learn to cast better if not here on the river?" Alden was beginning to enjoy the verbal lancing.

Charlie was beginning to enjoy it too. "Your back yard. It's the best place to develop technique."

"You forget I live in San Francisco. There are no back yards."

"Then try the casting ponds in the parks. Hell, they've got fisherman from five to a hundred and five casting in Golden Gate Park. There's always someone there to help a beginner."

"I'm too busy for that foolishness."

"But not too busy to come up here for three days, scare all our fish, and destroy my back rowing all day because you can't cast."

"You're getting paid for it. Now I know why you're so available. Do you verbally abuse all your clients?"

"No. Just the young, snotty ones...the arrogant ones who can't cast worth a damn." *Doreen was right. It is the young ones who give me so much grief. Why does respect skip a generation? Why do I put up with this? Why do I let this poor excuse of a fisherman get to me? I've guided worse.* "You're right. I am getting paid...almost enough to live on...so I have to put up with you. But what about you? What are you doing here? You're obviously not a serious fisherman. You don't pay attention to what I tell you or what I try to show you. You're obviously not enjoying the river."

"I'd enjoy it more if you'd put me on a fish. And I'd enjoy it more if you'd shut up, quit telling me what to do and let me concentrate."

"All right, how about a truce?" Feeling ashamed of himself, Charlie was genuinely contrite. His frown turned into a disarming smile. "You do the best you can, and I'll back-row you over the better lies. You try to enjoy being on the river, and I'll try to introduce you to fishing for Klamath steelhead without making a lesson and lecture out of it. What I'm saying is I'll try hard to get you into a fish, but if I don't, I'll still try to make the river a pleasant experience for you. Fair enough?"

"Fair enough." Alden also smiled. *Better be careful. I can't afford to have the Hawk turn adversarial.*

By early afternoon, with half their float completed, Alden was casting better and Charlie was feeling better, despite some pain in his shoulders. A soft west wind drifted in from a cloudless sky and rustled brittle leaves of birch trees along the river bank. The sun warmed his hands. As when he drove, he disdained the use of gloves. Through his bare hands on the oars, he wanted to feel the pulse of the river, the touch of its soul. And the Klamath finally responded. His client caught and released a dozen half-pounders, mini-steelhead that traveled downriver in schools. Although these immature fish of twelve to fifteen inches were scrappy fighters, Alden's tackle outmatched their valiant efforts to disengage. Alden didn't touch an adult fish.

As *Charlie's Pride* came out of a chute and rounded a bend, a different river sound greeted them—haunting and melodic but also eerie and wailing. Alden stood and gazed downstream. "What the hell is it?"

Charlie laughed. "It's our own Klamath siren...singing his way down the river."

"Like the mythical sirens of the seas?"

"Not quite. It's our Scottish guide, Wandering Willie. He's fishing below in Bigfoot's Bathtub...named for giant footprints seen occasionally in the sand. He's singing a Robbie Burns ballad, 'Braw Lads o Galla Water.' The canyon walls distort his voice so the sound seems not quite human. He's boated a steelhead there, and that's the song he sings when his favorite run produces." Charlie rested on his oars and let his boat drift with the current. "Willie always finishes his day with 'Auld Lang Syne.' You may hear him sing it when we take out."

"I'm not sure I want to. A balladeer for a guide. Next we'll have to put up with grand opera."

"Careful," Charlie chuckled. "Willie isn't real tolerant of an unappreciative audience. He had a client once who wasn't impressed with Willie's voice or choice of song. When his client asked him to stop, Willie stopped, then quietly rowed to shore, ordered his client out of the boat, and left the poor fellow stranded there madder'n a hornet. Willie finished the float by himself, singing all the way. His client had to scramble up the canyon to the highway in his waders and hitchhike back to Happy Camp.

"Fishing and singing are inseparable to Willie. He says he can't enjoy one without the other. Maybe he's right. I don't know. Seems out of place to me. Too much human noise intruding on natural river voices. Makes me wonder how humans would like it if a frog started croaking while the choir was singing in church on Sundays. Anyway, it seems to work for Willie. He catches a lot of steelhead, and his clients have a good time, as long as they like his singing or avoid adverse comment if they don't."

Alden pointed downriver. "I see them now. Sitting on shore, about halfway down the bar. Let's fish below them."

Charlie shook his head. "No way. We won't fish Bigfoot's Bathtub today."

"Why not?" Alden was impatient. "The water obviously holds fish and there's plenty of room."

"River courtesy." Charlie was irritated again. "We don't encroach, don't crowd in on a fisherman in a run, no matter how productive it is or how much room there is. When he's in it, it's his to fish until he finishes. All of it."

"But they're on shore. No one's fishing." Alden was sullen. *He's scolding me again.*

"They just released a steelhead. Willie's resting the run. We could stop here for lunch, watch them work the water, and have company while we eat." Charlie turned toward shore, still above Willie and his fisherman.

"No, Hawk. Let's keep going."

"Okay. You're the boss." In order to leave the unfished water undisturbed, Charlie redirected his boat toward the far bank. He waved to Willie as they drifted by, then cupped a hand around his mouth and called out, "Nice fish?"

"Aye," Willie responded with a thumbs-up gesture. "A gude fish. Fresh run hen. A braw leddy. A bonnie lass. And it's all over the top o' the water she was. Maybe eight pounds."

"What'd she take?" Charlie held his boat steady beyond the current.

"Aye, and I tell ye that, Hawk, ye soon be knowin' all me secrets," Willie teased. "Maybe she bit the Silver Hilton and maybe she bit somethin' else. Try them all, Hawk. Try them all. Aye, and this song's fer ye, Hawk…fer luck.

> *Come boat me o'er, come row me o'er*
> *Come boat me o'er to Charlie!*
> *I'll gie John Ross another bawbee*
> *To boat me o'er to Charlie."*

Willie's sonorous baritone seemed to float in the air as he repeated, *"Cha-a-a-r—le-e-e-e,"* holding the vowel sounds a long moment for extra effect. "Good luck to ye, Hawk, ye flinty-eyed, red-skinned, black tepee-topped auld fish monger. May the Klamath's own blood-striped leviathan bite for ye today. If he do, then it's a big jolt o' the Chivas ye put doon in front o' me tonight."

As Charlie let his boat slip into the current, he shouted back, "Not good enough, Willie. For a fish like that, it's the whole bottle for you. But it's got to be finished in one sitting. No leftovers."

"Aye, Hawk. The whole bottle in one sittin'. Fer that I dive into the river fer ye meself and fasten ye on to Bigfoot's own monster fishpet, the auld deil's buckie, Satan's imp hisself. And I do it quick before I remember it's the swimmin' I never learned. Aye and ye watch the turn o' yer oars in the big Dragon's Tooth rapid below. The dragon is orful mean and hungry, and his great snaggle tusk thrusts through the surface straight at ye when ye come off the chute. It's a turrible and chillin' sight. And it's an evil sight. That slimy divil's big bony protrusion do look like the horn o' a grand unicorn joustin' the mountain and sky. Come nigh to gore me poor boat in the arse two days ago. Puckers me hurdies just thinkin' about it."

"Thanks, Willie, thanks for the tip…and for the luck." Charlie tipped his hat to Willie as *Charlie's Pride* drifted below the bar.

On shore, Willie performed an exaggerated bow and doffed his tam o' shanter with a grand flourish. "See ye tonight, Hawk. See ye tonight. I be workin' on a powerful thirst."

BACK-ROWING through Rattlesnake Flats below Kanaha Hill was unproductive, and no fish held in the Wilson Creek run. Charlie's shoulders ached—*too much rowing*—and his arms cramped as the boat dipped into the Dragon's Tooth class III rapids below Buzzard Creek. The rapids maimed a few boats every year, particularly before low water, when standing waves surged over the dragon, out-muscled an unwary or inexperienced oarsman, and slammed his boat into the ragged, jutting hunk of projectile granite that gave the cataract its name. The trick was to turn the boat an abrupt ninety degrees at just the right instant. Too soon or too slow and the standing waves swamped the boat from the side. Too late and the dragon gnashed out at the stern below the water line. Now protruding from low water, the Dragon's Tooth was an ominous visual hazard, but less dangerous.

Charlie knew the rapids well. Years of experience gave him instinctive and precise timing, but his cramped muscles reacted late. His turn was slow and incomplete. The stern made it, but its flank grazed the dragon and slipped sideways to the current. Alden stumbled forward. His head banged into a stanchion, and his rod arced like a javelin into the river. He grabbed frantically at the gunnels. His left hand held, but his head and right shoulder pitched over the edge of the boat into the water. Charlie dropped his oars and scrabbled aft to help Alden. With too much weight on the downstream side, the boat listed dangerously and water poured in. To weight compensate, Charlie abandoned his original intention and fought to keep his body on the upstream side. With his feet, he punched at the unmanned oars. Slowly his boat slid out of the trough into placid water and righted itself. Alden came up coughing and pulled his upper body back into the boat. He gingerly massaged an angry welt on the side of his head. "What the hell happened?" he sputtered.

Charlie's chest heaved from exertion. "I...I was slow...too slow on the turn...the wave caught us sideways...."

"Damn fool! We almost swamped, and I've lost my rod."

"Yeah...because you didn't drop the rod...and...you didn't hold onto the seat...when we hit the chute." Charlie was still fighting to regain his breath.

"You didn't tell me," his client screeched.

"Alden..." The raptor's look returned to Charlie's eyes, and he blazed away, "...this is the third standing-wave rapids we've come through today. I instructed you on the first two. If you don't learn in-the-boat safety precautions any better than you learn out-of-the-boat casting techniques, we'll stop the boat right now. You're too much a hazard."

"I'm a hazard!" Alden was still screeching. "If you're getting too old to control a drift boat on the Klamath, maybe you're the hazard. If you can't handle it, get off the river. Before you kill somebody." It was cheap shot and he knew it. *Careful, don't push him too far.*

For an instant Charlie's face turned ashen under its light copper hue.

Alden caught the abrupt change in his guide, from anger to... what? Fear, the harbinger of weakness? Alden wondered why.

Alden had unknowingly triggered a flashback to Charlie's brush crew accident. Its effect was brief but intense and defeating. Charlie slowly regained his composure and flipped a bailing tin to Alden. "Here," he said in a subdued voice, "get some water out of the boat and we'll put in for lunch at Wingate Bar."

Their bitter exchange and the after-effect of sudden adrenaline surges drained the anger from both of them. Alden cheerfully accepted the menial task of bailing, as Charlie redirected his boat back into the current and headed downriver.

FOR most of lunch both guide and angler were silent. Afterward they stood and watched two men wearing face masks, air tubes and wet suits operate a dredge at the tail of Wingate Bar. Each of the men maneuvered a long suction hose, maybe four inches in diameter, along the river bottom. Behind them three bright yellow pontoons about ten feet long floated their dredge equipment. At the front, a gas engine spewed blue smoke, churned, sputtered, and coughed, creating a powerful suction in the hoses, like a giant vacuum cleaner cleansing the river bottom. At the rear, a wide screen trap captured small rocks and gravel sucked through the hoses. A long grayish-brown plume of silt billowed downstream from the dredge, like the tail of some giant serpent gorging on the flesh of the river. Periodically the dredgers dove and then resurfaced, as they brought up and stacked to the side larger rocks which were too big for their hoses.

"They process the sediments…all the way to bedrock if they can," Charlie explained. "And they leave behind scores of un-filled troughs. We call them dredgers' graves. Their potholes and trenches are sometimes ten feet deep. You have to be very careful wading. Even when the water is this clear, the dredgers' graves aren't that easy to spot. You can easily dunk into one way over your head."

Alden was curious. "Are the dredges effective?"

"Very."

"Do they find gold?"

"Sometimes a lot. These portable dredges operate like the huge, floating dredge-houses operated by turn-of-the-century placer miners, only more efficiently. It's wet and backbreaking work, but dredgers can make good money if they don't drown and their backs hold up."

"The engine noise is deafening," Alden said.

"Only on the surface. Below the surface they say it's a differ-ent world. Very quiet. All the dredgers hear is a tinkling sound of pebbles sucked into their hoses. Sometimes, when the dredgers dive deep, they actually see gold flakes glittering in a long, nar-row ribbon along the river bottom, like an underwater path of gold sprinkled by a human hand rather than the caprice of Klam-ath currents. Yes, sometimes the river is uncommonly kind, even to those who disturb her tranquil places and plunder her hidden treasure. There's not a lot of gold left in the river, but it seems to concentrate along these long bars."

"How do they separate the gold from all that gravel?"

Charlie laughed and pointed to the trap. "Same way the first prospectors did: manually. They use old-fashioned pans to sift through deposits that accumulate on the screen in the trap. Gold flakes are the heaviest sediments, and they settle to the bottom of the pan. Modern technology never has developed a better way."

Alden was seriously interested. *This beats fishing,* he thought. "Where does the gold come from?" he said.

Charlie pointed to a far off cluster of peaks, barely visible above and beyond a protective ridge. "From up there, in the high mountains. During rains, gold washes into the river from nearly every small stream or gulch. Only a few dredgers work the river now, and they say that every year the Klamath system replenishes as much as they take out. They just don't always know where to find it."

"Fascinating," Alden said. "Sounds like you've done it."

Charlie nodded. "Sure, I had gold fever...once. Sooner or later it infects everyone born on the Klamath. But I haven't dredged. My Hupok ancestors believed evil things happened to anyone who disturbed the river that way." Charlie was embarrassed to reveal his adherence to an old tribal superstition. "I did pan for gold...when I was a teenager. For two summers. But not on the river. My father and I worked several small streams far back in the Siskiyou Mountains.

"He spoke often of a Hupok legend about an ancient, lost river of gold which was part of the orogeny of the Klamath National Forest. He said his grandfather once possessed several large gold nuggets found in the river. But its location was lost to the Hupoks more than a century ago. How ironic that a tribe that coveted wealth so highly never recognized value in their yellow baubles until it was too late, and the secret of their source was buried in the failing memory of the tribe's last historian. To them their golden nuggets were only small pebbles of an inferior color. The first bearded gold seekers stripped my ancestors of their few gold possessions but never found the source."

"And you and your father found the source?" Alden asked, trying not to sound excited.

"No." Charlie's eyes reflected a strange melancholy. "If we had, I wouldn't jeopardize an old age of peace, comfort, and respect by continuing to defy the Klamath and deny my own physical decline."

"But you learned the national forest when you prospected for gold?"

"Even earlier, when I was a small boy."

"And you know it well?"

"No one knows it better."

"Will you take me there?" Alden's eyes were penetrating and calculating.

Charlie was caught momentarily off guard, and then shook his head. "No, my gold-seeking days are over. Long over. If there are riches up there, and I doubt it, they no longer interest me."

"It's not gold I'm interested in."

"What is it then?"

Alden hesitated. "It's the growers and their marijuana plantations. I want to see them, and I know you're familiar with their sites and their operations."

Charlie was silent and inscrutable for a long time. He looked northward to the mountains. A shadow crossed his features, and he looked back. A raptor's fierce gaze again glared at Alden, who shivered and dropped his eyes. Charlie's glare was relentless, and there was fury in his voice when he finally spoke. "Now, tell me what you know about me, who you really are, and why you want to see the plantations. Tell me all of it. If you don't, your journey to the Klamath and our conversation end right here, right now."

Alden regained eye contact and proceeded, this time without hesitation. "Okay, you're entitled. I'll start with me. I'm not much of a fisherman. You figured that out right away. And I'm not here to fish. I suspect you guessed that also. I'm a feature writer, and a damn good one. I generally get the information I want, and I'm willing to pay for it. I've been commissioned to do a story on the marijuana fields hidden in the national forests of northern California. There's big money in this, if I can get into the camps and do the story from the inside. I'll pay you five thousand dollars to take me there, another five thousand when you get me out." Alden paused. Charlie remained impassive and silent, and Alden continued, "I know you spent two years in the camps working for the growers, came out, and haven't gone back."

Charlie still smoldered. "How do you know that?"

"Look, Hawk, it's no secret. You're well known here. I have an associate who spent two evenings at Tony Fisheyes a month ago. You weren't there. When the beer and whiskey are flowing, there's a lot of loose tongues in that tavern. They gossip about everyone on the river, and there's a lot of talk about you."

"That goddam Tommy Two Stumps," Charlie exclaimed. "But why me? Why select me? Former plantation workers are scattered all up and down the river. Tommy knows them all. And he's quick to gossip about all of them. Why me? Surely you have other names."

"I have. But I liked what I heard about your Indian heritage. I figured you'd be a better guide."

"How do you know I won't turn you in to the growers, collect a higher bounty?"

Alden was cautious with his answer. "Because I know about your daughter, Hawk, your younger daughter. I know she was killed in a car accident at college...on her way home from a pot party. They say she and her friends started on marijuana about the time you went into the mountains. I figure you've got good cause to hate the growers and no reason to turn me in, even for money."

Another shadow crossed Charlie's features. "Yeah, I hate the growers. But why should I stick my neck out for you? The plantations and their camps are dangerous. And you and I don't get along very well. I don't like you, I don't like your bringing my daughter into this, and I don't think I can trust you."

"I know you don't like me. I know I did a miserable job of building cordiality between us, and I know you have no reason to trust me. But I know you need the money. And I think you know your days of guiding on the river are numbered. Think about it. Don't decide now. Let me know tomorrow. Pick me up at the tackle shop. We can spend the day in the mountains. No one

need know. And do the same the next day. And for the rest of the
week if you're not booked. We can fix it so everyone thinks we're
on the river. You don't have to go into the camps. Just get me
there, point me in the right direction and give me some names if
you can. I need to interview some of the workers."

Charlie shook his head, and raised his hand as if to ward off
a physical blow. "And what if the growers catch us? Their camps
are patrolled. There are people there who know me. We'll be
questioned."

"I've thought of that too. I'll introduce myself as a buyer
from New York. I've done my homework, and I can carry it off.
The growers here are selling mostly in the west and in Chicago.
They're being squeezed by competing growers from Mexico.
They'll jump at a chance to sell into the big eastern markets."

Charlie was silent a long moment.

"Just think about it, Hawk," Alden urged.

Charlie looked again to the northern mountains, as if he
sought an answer where the Klamath ridges pyramided to a blue
horizon far up Clear Creek valley. When he turned again to look
at Alden, his hawk's glare was gone. His eyes reflected only sadness and uncertainty. "All right, Alden, I'll think about it. I swore
I'd never go back...but it might work."

Alden nodded his head, but remained instinctively silent as
Charlie turned a third time and looked deeper into the Siskiyous.

What did he see there? All the peaks and valleys he once knew
so well, images fixed in his mind, but not visible from Wingate
Bar. Preston Peak was back there and its sisters, El Capitan and
Copper Mountain, guardians of the White Feather Mine. So were
the remote, hidden, mystical places seldom seen because box can-
yons and thundering falls denied access to all but the most perse-
vering...places like the Devil's Punch Bowl, Cyclone Gap, Dark
Canyon, and the valley of Hurdy-Gurdy Creek, where Charlie
and his father once panned for gold. Then there were the places
he remembered with anger, where the growers tended their illicit
crops on secluded flanks of high ridges that had no names.

He knew the Klamath provided a nexus between his past and

present—the dreams of a boy, the pride of a young man, the shame that followed, and the troubled search for contentment in middle age. But his images provided no revelations about his future. All landscapes, those before him and those in his mind, remained mute and challenged him to find his own way through fortune's maze.

When he finally spoke again, his gaze stayed fixed on the horizon. He spoke slowly and with hesitation and distraction, as if Alden weren't there. "I'm linked to the oldest river system in the western United States...the Klamath and its interdependent and inseparable trinity, the river, its mountains, and its forests.

"Timeless.

"Endless.

"Sometimes kind and generous. Sometimes harsh and unforgiving.

"Always my joy, but always my sorrow. For all my life."

Charlie paused, dropped his gaze from the horizon, and spoke very softly, "Will my destiny also be forever bound to the Klamath?"

When he finally turned to face Alden, he smiled. "Tomorrow, you'll have your answer. For today, although I have equipment you could use, there'll be no more fishing. We'll float through and take out early." He laughed then. "It'll be easier on you, a lot easier on me, and I'm sure our fish will appreciate it."

TAWASKEENA
Where the River Sings

SEPTEMBER BROUGHT SHORTENED DAYS to the Klamath, even shorter in the gorge where the sun arrived late and departed quickly. In the half-light, half-shadow of a day not entirely spent, Charlie backed his van and boat trailer down the steep gravel drive leading to his cabin, relying on habit to remind him when to stop. Then he exited the van, rubbed his aching shoulders, walked back to his drift boat, and frowned at its river-worn appearance. *Age weary...like me.* His drawn face relaxed into a smile as he again patted the transom sign and spread his fingers along its flaking letters—an evening ritual. *Doreen's artistry needs fresh paint. It also fades with time.* Stepping forward, he ran his palm along a ragged twelve-inch groove, freshly inflicted courtesy of his morning encounter with the Dragon's Tooth. A soft whistle escaped his lips. *By the river spirits that was close. A graze just above the water line. Paint scraped and siding gouged, but no serious damage to repair. The river forgives me another mistake.*

Uncoupling the boat trailer from the van, he rested its hitch on a wooden mooring that tilted the boat so water could drain. Then he removed his flag, washed down his boat, and encased it in a waterproof cover. It was another ritual he followed at the close of every working day, no matter how late the hour, how great his fatigue, how sore his body, or how troubled his state of mind. Years before he'd done the same with his logging trucks. As with his trucks, his boat was his livelihood, and he took good care of it. Surprising how many guides didn't bother.

Finished with his cleanup, he looked longingly at a narrow opening in the forest beside his cabin and then raised his eyes to the sky. *Plenty of daylight left. And I need to steer my mind away from Alden and his proposal.* Suppressing his fatigue and ignoring his shoulder pain, he rubbed at the stiffness in his left leg and headed toward the path.

When his work permitted, which was more frequently now, he liked to walk down to the river. He spent quiet evenings there with memories far more pleasant than those that greeted him at dawn. He felt less lonely with the Klamath beside him and its dense riparian growth around him. It wasn't far, maybe 300 yards down a switchback trail that wound through Douglas fir and big-leaf maples. During Indian summer the changing season left no imprint on the stately firs, but maple leaves boasted autumn's artistry in a yellow and brown mottling, which late-day sunlight mixed and displayed in brilliant orange. He'd built his trail, not by hewing it out but simply by following the same course to the river year after year. His path was like those of his ancestors—carved by moccasined feet. How many evenings had it taken him? Probably a thousand.

Now he shared his path only with deer and other forest creatures. The soft earth in front of him was pockmarked with their tracks. As a young couple, he and Doreen had raced down the path together, like young deer in springtime. Now he limped down alone. *Like an old buck in winter.*

His path ended at a bar of pebbles and sand that stretched for a hundred yards adjacent to the river's near shore. Flooded by high water during spring, the bar was fully exposed when the river receded, generally by midsummer. A large black lava boulder lodged at the head of the bar. Neatly form-fit to hold a seated person, the boulder's southwest face absorbed afternoon sun, holding heat until long after evening shadows enveloped the bar. He shuffled across the sand and sat there, listening to the river. Thermal heat radiated from the boulder and eased the ache in his shoulders.

From his sun rock he surveyed a long back eddy where, even

in late season, a powerful surge of water foamed off a rock ledge and forced part of the current to reverse and flow slowly back upstream. His private beach owed its existence to detritus washed up by the back eddy. But by autumn the swirling sediments were gone. Now maple leaves blanketed the Klamath. Some rode high on the surface like miniature golden gondolas, some floated dull and lifeless just beneath the surface. The back eddy captured many of autumn's discards, and they swept by him in long, elliptical paths. First they drifted upriver. Then, snared at the current edge, they raced back down and into the eddy again. The process was a continuous repetition, broken only when an evening breeze gusted and whisked leaves who could still ride the wind far out into the main current where they escaped the back eddy's contrary pull. *Just like me. Discarded and trapped in the damned backwash of this river, until something I can't control pushes me out of it.*

He knew the back eddy washed ten feet deep next to the rock ledge. Later in autumn, if any remnants made it that far, spawned-out king salmon held there, spent and dying in gentle water. As their strength ebbed and their flesh softened, a killing fungus invaded and destroyed their body tissues. While yet living, they turned a deathly grayish color and hovered motionless in the slow contra-current, nosed downstream against it. Their gills processed just enough oxygen to sustain their last hours. Only death remained for ghostly specters of the Klamath to complete their role in the river's chain of life. On those evenings, if he lingered late enough, he might see raccoons come down to feast on the flesh of dead salmon and fight among themselves over the choicest bits.

He missed the family of river otters who once made their home along the back eddy, growing fat and sleek on their rich fare of fish. They were gone now, victims of some trapper who had poached his private beach. Or perhaps they just moved on when the salmon and steelhead runs diminished.

What he missed most were beach evenings with Doreen. Those evenings were relics of the past, lost to his present, spawned during his pride years and frozen in time long ago, before his world turned solemn. Images haunted him. He shut his eyes and summoned them.

————————

FROM SHORE THEY WATCH a family of river otters at play. A smooth, narrow chute through a ledge above the back eddy provides the otters with their own private water slide. In pairs they toboggan down the chute. They clutch each other, chatter noisily, and plunge—sometimes head first, sometimes feet first—off the ledge and into the river below. "They always put on a special show for us," he tells her, squeezing her hand.

"Like children when they know they have an audience," she says.

Tiring of play, the otters scramble out onto their favorite rocks. The younger ones stand upright on their webbed feet, scratch their bellies with their fore-flippers, look solemn, and, with unblinking eyes, stare at the two intruding humans. The adults lie motionless on the rocks locked in a concupiscent embrace. "Look Charlie, those two imps are mocking us," she says.

He knows she loves early September best. Most of the river crowds are gone then, but the waters of the Klamath are still warm and inviting. They've come down early, before sunlight leaves the gorge. After the otters swim away, she tries to entice him into an evening swim. Beckoning him, she speaks in a husky voice "Come in with me? Now? Swim with me, Charlie the Hawk." Barefoot and brazen, she stands facing him with a wicked smile and begins to disrobe. She does it slowly, with purpose and without inhibition. She unbuckles and unzips, wriggles shorts and panties to her ankles, gracefully steps free, bends to pick them up, straightens and throws them at him with a throaty laugh. "Like what you see, Charlie?" she teases. "Then, what about this?" Hands on her hips, she raises to her toes and twirls a half-turn. Stretching her hands behind her and glancing back over her shoulder, she unties and removes her halter top. Then she completes her turn and takes a step toward him. Bare toes touch moccasins, and she drapes the garment, warm and dewy, over his head, letting the tips of her breasts brush his shirt front, chuckling when she senses an instinctive shudder begin inside him.

He can tease too. "You're backwards, Doreen. You always do it backwards, pants first. Most women go halter first."

"Sure, Charlie. And how is it you're such an expert? I think you enjoy it more pants first. This way I know you can't grab me when your hands are full of pants." She laughs, and before he can master the juggling act with her clothes, she's in the water, diving to the deepest part of the back eddy. Her lithe body knifes through the water, then lunges and arcs at the surface with a dolphin's grace.

Content to stay on the beach, he dodges her attempts to splash him, listens to her peals of laughter and watches her paddle gaily about the back eddy. Her long black hair streams on the surface behind her, as lustrous and glistening in sunlight as the skin of the elegant otters who frolicked there only a short time before. "Watch me, Charlie," she calls. She floats on her back, thrusts her hips high in the water, clasps her hands across her stomach, purses her lips and pinches her nose trying to imitate an otter's mock solemnity, and then blows soft, guttural coughing sounds into the water. Barely decipherable, the sounds seem to say, "I love you, Charlie the Hawk." Then she clears her voice and calls, "Who am I, Charlie?"

"You need more whiskers and less bosom, and you're a bit heavy in the bottom," he teases. He relishes his internal sensations, as her natural grace and abandonment in the water delight and tantalize him. More than that, it makes him happy to see her happy. "I love to watch you in the water, Doreen. And I know who you are. You're a river creature, my beautiful river creature. You're living proof of God's intention...your God or my ancestors', it makes no difference."

She's aware of her effect on him. It excites and pleases her. She knows and accepts that his first love is the Klamath. In private moments like these she shows him her love of the river in ways words cannot. She knows the joining of their feelings about the river strengthens love bonds between them more than just a physical joining of bodies. She repeats the otter sounds and then calls to him again, "What did I say, Charlie?"

"You said *g grrg grg grrggll grr grgg,*" he responds.

"Beast! Listen to me. Carefully."

He cocks his head and cups a hand to his ear.

A second time she repeats the sounds. "What did I say?"

"You said you love me," he calls.

"That's what I said, Charlie. Now, what do you say? Tell me, Hawk. I want to hear it."

At first he's reluctant. Then, sheepishly, he finally expels a *"g grrg grg grrgll."*

"In English, Tamiko."

As always when she uses his childhood Indian name, he feels a surge of pride. He stands at river's edge and calls out, "I love you, Doreen."

"I know, Charlie. But I've always known. I want the rest of the river to know. Tell me louder, Charlie." Turning over, she swims toward shore.

"I love you, Doreen," he shouts.

"Louder, Charlie, louder." Her toes touch bottom now, and she can almost stand. "I want the world to know."

He cups both hands about his mouth and swells his lungs until he's sure they'll burst. "I LOVE YOU, DOREEN!" His words explode into the air. Echoes bounce off canyon walls, "I love you Doreen...love you Doreen...love Doreen," until they fade into soft, evanescent whispers downriver: *"Doreen...Doreen... Doreen."*

She moves forward. When the river shelves, she steps onto a shallow ledge and rises slowly until the back eddy swirls about her knees, creating miniature whirlpools in the broken current. Water cascades from her head and shoulders. A rivulet courses between her breasts, down her stomach and loses itself in the dark, silky shadows below. Her hair falls about her in gleaming, satiny strands. She extends her arms and beckons. "Then come show me, Tamiko. Show me now."

He can stand the swelling heat within him no longer, and he strips off his shirt, popping a button in the process.

Laughing at his clumsy efforts to disengage from his clothing, she transfers her hands to her hips, showing him her impatience.

Fumbling with an unruly belt, he stumbles and nearly falls trying to step from his trousers and kick free from his moccasins in the same motion.

"Quickly, Charlie, come quickly," she calls, again opening her arms.

As if exploding from a fountain, water splashes about him as he strides through the back eddy to join her. Then their arms lock their bodies together. Their eyes lock their hearts and souls together. "Now...be slow, Tamiko," she whispers, her voice husky and halting. "Please...be slow."

SPENT and happy, entangled in each other and relishing the sun's warmth, they rest on a sloping rock shelf at river's edge. Their cuddling rock they call it, and they use their clothing to buffer the harshness of its surface. After the late-day sun dries them, she reaches for his shirt and hands it to him. "And now," she commands, "brush the sand from me, Charlie, and please be thorough...particularly here." With her free hand she points to her breasts.

They kneel facing each other. She closes her eyes and arches her back with her hands clasped behind her head. He dabs gently, first at her face then descending over her neck and shoulders and beyond. At the touch of soft flannel against her skin, she mouths a throaty hum of pleasure, like a kitten purring. When the fabric brushes them, her nipples announce her renewed arousal. He pauses a moment to cup each breast tenderly with his shirt-covered hands.

"Don't stop," she sighs.

"No grain of sand untouched," he whispers.

She sighs again as he moves slowly downward, applying slight pressure through the flannel with his fingertips in a series of lingering caresses.

"Other side...please." She breathes her words, pivots on her knees and stretches. Again arching her back, she raises her arms and extends her hands palms forward, as if offering a prayer to the setting sun.

"Not much sand back here," he whispers.

"Don't be so literal, Charlie. Just stroke me." Again her voice is husky, this time insistent and not halting.

He complies, his hands and fingertips again working where they're most needed—nape of neck, shoulders, upper back, loins, buttocks, outer thighs, calves. "Am I done now, my love?"

"No, my love. Now my feet," she commands. Rotating again, she lies on her back, lifts her legs and extends her feet into his trembling hands.

The sight is too much for him. "Enough, Doreen," he cries out, as if in pain. "I...I...I have to stop."

"No, Tamiko, you have to keep going."

Throwing his shirt to the sand, he gasps and falls forward into her outstretched arms. Again their two bodies fuse as one, wrapped in fading sunlight and dancing shadows.

DESPITE the sun's departure and a cooling late-day breeze, they remain unclothed. It's from each other they draw what warmth they need. She sits nestled between his muscular legs, her back and head resting against his broad chest. She retrieves a hairbrush from a shorts pocket and passes it back over her shoulder. A sigh and slight shake of her head convey her request. Both are silent and pensive while he brushes the lingering damp from her hair.

"Your hair is soft...so soft," he whispers, breaking their silence as he returns her hairbrush. Then, using them like a comb, he strokes his fingers through the full length of her hair, flaring it at the ends. Carefully he separates the strands, left and right. Then he presses his lips to the top of her head and brushes them down the narrow furrow where the strands part. She trembles, and he repeats the light caress, this time pursing his lips and exhaling so she can feel a warm, delicate breath. "It's the color of Indian hair but so much softer...particularly there," he says as he sweeps her hair over him, moves his lips to the nape of her neck, and kisses her there, before again exhaling, this time with a more heated and powerful breath.

Again she trembles.

"Why do you like for me to brush it?" he asks.

Her voice is drowsy. "Because it comforts me...and it makes me feel loved. More even than a body caress. I love the feel of your body against mine when you are brushing me. I can feel your muscles contract and expand. They show me you are strong, and they show me you are gentle." She sighs and is thoughtful for a minute. "Do you know what else I love about your body next to mine?"

"What, Doreen? Tell me."

"I've never told you before."

"Tell me. Tell me now."

She hesitates. "Maybe I shouldn't."

"Please. Tell me. I want to know everything that pleases you."

"It's your Indian skin."

"My Indian skin?" He's perplexed. "You know I'm only half-Indian."

"Yes, your beautiful, coppery, half-Indian skin."

"Its color?" He laughs. "You like the color of my skin?"

"No, silly. It's because you...you have no hair, except...except in that one place. It's the smoothness of your body I love. And, when you hold me like this, here beside the river you love beyond reason, I can feel your emotions surge through me, through all of me. Your body always feels so natural to me, smells so fresh and clean." She nestles deeper against him and breathes in, nostrils flared. "I can't imagine any woman being held like this by a man with a hairy body...*uggh*."

"I wish I'd known about this a long time ago. Think of all the conquests I missed because I wasn't aware of my racial advantage."

"Randy brute." She reaches back and prods him in the ribs. "I knew I shouldn't have revealed my secret."

"But I'm glad you did. I promise not to take advantage of it...except with you. Here, feel all of me." Disengaging his hands from her hair, he encircles her with his arms over hers, grips the entire length of her legs with his, burrows his head and chin into the long smooth curve of her neck and shoulder, kisses her on the cheek, letting her feel the warm, soft wetness of his tongue, and whispers, "You are now wrapped head to toe in the skin of one adoring half-Indian." Then he squeezes—hard.

"Don't ever let me go, Tamiko," she gasps.

"I won't...river creature. Not ever."

"Not even when we're old?"

"Not even then."

"I can't bear the thought of being old."

"Then don't think about it."

"I won't. Maybe if you always hold me like this, we'll never grow old."

He laughs. "I thought you weren't going to think about it."

"I'm sorry. I can't help it. Maybe we won't grow old."

"No, Doreen, we will grow old. Like all living things."

"Don't say that, Tamiko. Don't spoil it. I want it to stay like this. Forever."

"I want it, too. But it can't."

"But we can wish it, can't we?"

"Yes."

"And we can dream it, can't we?"

"Yes."

"And we can pretend it?"

"Yes."

"Okay. Let's pretend it will be always like this. You hold me. And we never grow old."

"I'll hold you...my river creature. All through the night... right here if you want me to."

"No, Tamiko. Not just through the night. Hold me always. Promise? Promise to hold me always?"

"Always." He kisses her cheek again. "I promise to hold you always. Until eternity dawns, the rivers all run dry, and the Klamath no longer hurries to the sea."

NOW, SEPTEMBER IDYLLS were only memories, Charlie's most cherished memories. Passing years had driven away warm autumn evenings together, but not their place in his heart or among the images in his mind.

Now, Doreen was in Eureka by the sea, and he was alone on the river—and they weren't young anymore. On the few weekends she came to make sure he kept his home tidy, she said she was too busy or too tired in the legs to follow him down to the river. So, on warm autumn evenings like this, when work permitted, Charlie pursued a solitary mission into his past. He sat motionless on his sun rock and looked at the empty rock beyond, where an eternal embrace was once Doreen's promised destiny. He remembered and was sad. He wondered if she remembered and was sad. He struggled to recall his best memories. Did he have another? His face lightened and he smiled. Yes, he did. It was one of their last evenings together at the back eddy, before time and tribulation intervened.

———————

AS THEY REST side-by-side and listen to the Klamath rush and babble, she asks, "Do you think your Hupok ancestors came here?"

He nods his head. "Yes. Because of all the river sounds, they called this place Tawaskeena, which means 'where the river sings'."

"You've not told me its Indian name before."

"Because I no longer think of places by their Indian names."

"That's sad, Charlie. Tawaskeena is such a pretty name."

"I remember most names. I just don't think to use them... not even with you."

"Did your people swim in the back eddy?"

"I'm sure they did."

"Just like we do?"

"Yes."

"And made love here at Tawaskeena?"

"No-o-o," he laughs. "They came here to bathe."

She prods him in the ribs and sighs. "Not very romantic."

"No, but necessary."

For a moment they are both silent. Then she reaches over and clasps his hands in hers. "Were they as happy as we?" she asks.

He's drowsy. "Who?"

"Your Hupok ancestors, silly. Were they happy?"

"Yes, I think so. Their life wasn't easy, but they were happy."

"Good. I like knowing you're descended from happy people. I wouldn't want a gloomy half-Indian for a husband."

"Do you think I'm gloomy?"

"Sometimes. When you're driving too much." She turns to face him. Touching his face with her hands, she looks at him intently. "No, I don't think you're gloomy. Fierce sometimes. When you look like a hawk searching for his prey."

"Do I look fierce now?" He grimaces and tries to look fierce.

"No, you look like a man who's spoiled rotten and is suffering from recent and excessive gratification of his senses." She releases his hands, rocks back on her haunches, and stretches.

He reaches for her then. "And you look like an overindulged woman who just enjoyed gratification as much as I...and who is now ready to enjoy some more."

"No. Go away." She slaps his hands and boxes his ears playfully. "Someone might see."

"You didn't used to worry about others' eyes." He grasps her hands and presses them to his lips.

"That was before the river became so popular."

"And you certainly weren't worried a few minutes ago."

"That was different."

"Why different?"

"We were in the water. The river protected us."

"So, let's go back in the water."

She shivers. "No, Charlie, the sun is gone."

"Then I'll tell the sun to come back." He beckons to a lavender glow in the western horizon.

"Will you do that for me, Charlie? Make the sun return?"

"If it will make you happy, I'll tell the sun never to set."

"Do it, Tamiko. And we'll stay in the water forever."

"But, how will we live?"

"I don't know. Somehow. You're the one who always says the river will sustain us."

"We'll shrivel up like a couple of prunes."

Giggling, she tries to make a shriveled face. "Could you still love me as a prune?" She draws his hands to her face.

Cupping her face in his hands, he studies her features for a moment, as if trying to make up his mind. Then he scrunches up his face to copy hers. "Yes, could you me?"

"I don't know." She returns her hands to his face. "You really look awful as a prune." Then she pinches his puckered cheeks and looks at him wickedly. "But I shouldn't make quick judgments. Further investigation is required." Leaning forward, she kisses him tentatively on each check. "You don't taste too bad for a prune. I need to try some more." She brushes her lips over each of his closed eyelids, nibbles hungrily at his ears, letting him feel her teeth until he grimaces, and then samples his lips in a lingering kiss. *"Mmm.* Pretty tasty for a prune. But I need to know more."

"What's that?"

"Can prunes make love?"

"I don't think so."

"Why not?"

"Because their skin is too sticky."

She thinks about that for a moment. "At least that's better than too hairy. We could stick together and float down the river...all the way to the sea."

That gives them both the giggles. Convulsed with laughter, they embrace. She clamps her legs about his waist and draws herself to him. *"Mmm.* You don't feel sticky. Just nice. Nice and smooth. This way I can hold you too."

"I thought you were worried about being seen."

"Not any more. Let the whole world see."

Their laughter fades to an occasional chuckle and then they are quiet. They move slowly and rhythmically for a very long time. Until a powerful shudder engulfs both of them and expands into a lingering sigh that exhales from deep inside. Then they hold each other tightly, without moving. Until their muscles cramp. Wanting it to last forever.

In a sudden burst of energy, she springs to her feet, tosses her head first to one side and then the other. Her hair swirls about her shoulders. Ebbing light behind her accentuates the refulgent sheen of her body. She glows like a luminescent silhouette. "Was it like this with Adam and Eve, Charlie?"

"What do you mean?"

"In the Garden of Eden. Did Adam and Eve have a river?"

"I don't think so."

"I think they must have."

"Why?"

"To be happy without clothes, they must have had a river."

"They had a snake."

She grimaces. "*Uggh*, no wonder they got into trouble. I don't see how anyone could be happy with a snake."

"They thought the snake made them happy with his ideas... about the apple."

"I'm glad we don't have a snake with any crazy ideas. We don't have a snake, do we Tamiko?"

"No, river creature...just a river in our Garden of Eden. And our cuddling rock."

"It's too bad Adam and Eve didn't have a river with a place to cuddle, instead of that garden with an apple tree. Snakes can't live on a rock in a river."

"And people can't make love in an apple tree."

"Then I'm glad we're not like Adam and Eve. Except for that no clothes part. Sometimes that's nice."

He rises to his feet and reaches for her. "That's always nice."

She slips into his arms. "So maybe we are like Adam and Eve. Naked, shameless, and quick to succumb to temptation!"

"Except we have to put our clothes back on and return to reality." He breaks their long embrace and reaches for his clothes.

"Do we have to, Tamiko?" She's dreamy and reluctant.

"Yes."

"Why?"

His smile is roguish, as he brushes grains of sand from her flanks with his shirt and pats her bare round bottom. "Because, most lovely, radiant, and rare of river creatures, sometimes even prunes have to eat, sleep, and rise before dawn to go to work."

"Okay, if we must," she sighs her acceptance. Then she thumps him on the chest and gathers her clothes in her arms.

Still barefoot and unclothed, they chase each other back up the path and into lingering twilight. Behind them their shadows dance, and their voices echo back to fill the gorge with laughter.

———

CHARLIE SAT ON HIS sun rock at Tawaskeena and tried to remember more. But he couldn't. He closed his eyes and felt stored heat seep into him and sedate him. His mind languished.

He listened to the river and absorbed its moods. The Klamath roared as it swept over submerged ledges, and he suffered the river's frenzy. Spume-crowned waves slapped high on lava boulders, and he welcomed the river's abandon. Spray hissed against an exposed stone face, gathered in droplets and spattered onto time-worn rocks below, and he endured the river's anguish. Gentle currents gurgled and chuckled in the back eddy, and he relished the river's delight. When he listened very carefully, he heard the soft wash at water's edge ripple along the beach like an ocean finally at rest, and he embraced the river's serenity.

It was a privileged evening, and he listened to water ouzels sing from high in the mossy oak trees that supplied their spring nesting material. Their songs were haunting and beautiful. Clear and uplifting. Full of hope and happiness. Messages of joy from tiny bodies bursting with rapture. He marveled that such plain and drab, gray-colored birds could fill the gorge with such majestic sound. Their songs cheered him, reminded him of laughter from the past.

Then he remembered again.

And memory was a physical ache within him.

When the ouzels stopped, he thought he heard Doreen's lilting laugh from the back eddy. Hopefully he leaned forward and opened his eyes to greet her.

But she wasn't there.

Then he wept.

And his tears streamed down his cheeks and dripped into the sand.

TONY FISHEYES

*N*OW *NEEDING TO* escape his memories, Charlie changed into clean Levis and a new flannel shirt and headed back outside to his van. *I won't stay long at Tony Fisheyes*, he thought. *I have a lot to think about and a decision to make...and I should call Doreen before I make it. I won't get drawn into storytelling. "Fantasies and fables of tavern fishermen," she calls it.*

When he didn't work, he dined alone in his cabin and tried to stay busy to escape his loneliness. He built furniture, wrote to his daughter, tied flies, mostly brightly colored patterns of his own design, did crossword puzzles, and continued reading habits developed during long years of self-education.

When his public education ended with high school, he had continued a private education. Books were his teachers. With the same intense curiosity and single-minded purpose that drove his boyhood's upriver quests he sought the knowledge and experience of others. He read slowly, so he absorbed slowly. Word by word. Page by page. To read, he stole a few hours from a driving week already too long or from a family Sunday. He read on nasty winter days, when the wind howled and wind-driven sleet stung exposed flesh like pellets from an air gun, days when no one worked outside and even forest creatures cowered and sought day-long shelter from the storm. He read, not for social or economic advancement, for he knew his life was irrevocably committed to the Klamath, but simply to please himself. His interest in what came from the hearts and minds of others never flagged, was never trivialized.

Now he read for relaxation and entertainment, as well as enlightenment. His handcrafted bookshelves lined the walls of his cabin, floor to ceiling. They sagged under a crowded load of *Time* magazines, twenty-five years of *National Geographic* issues, and an extensive collection of worn editions of fine books, from Schopenhauer to Dickens to Hemingway, all secured from San Francisco's used bookstores on his annual trip to the city. A special section was reserved for the complete works covering his favorite characters from more contemporary literature—Pogo and Calvin & Hobbes.

The occasional client who visited Charlie's cabin was amazed to find a literary host. A fishing guide who reads philosophy and the classics—and the comics? And a half-Indian at that? Why is he guiding fishermen for an income barely above the poverty level? Charlie frequently asked himself the same question.

Even Doreen scolded him, "Charlie, you should read less, talk to people more."

He had his answer ready, "No, Doreen. People die. Words live forever. Books are immortality's promise."

On non-working days, he shunned the company of others and avoided Tony Fisheyes. On those days he felt low in spirits and sensitive to the age difference that separated him from younger guides. Their youthful banter seemed artificial, and it irritated rather than cheered him. He sensed their embarrassment and their uncomfortable feelings—for him, feelings they didn't know how to express. But he felt their pity. He saw it in their eyes. He recognized it in what they didn't say. It was suppressed by a veneer of high spirits, but it impaired the relaxed naturalness of any group joviality. By staying home on non-working days, he avoided their pity.

When he worked, his spirits improved and he sought company. Then he dined at Tony Fisheyes and enjoyed the carefree congeniality of younger guides. Then he didn't feel their pity so much. When his working days didn't produce a steelhead, other guides shared his disappointment on a sympathetic basis. Sympathy for fishlessness was different from pity for middle-age jobless-

ness. Every guide experienced long periods of steelhead drought.
Not catching fish was nearly as companionable a circumstance as
catching fish and often more entertaining. It was a bittersweet
companionship, for he regretted he didn't have a son, and he
searched the earnest, fresh faces around him, trying to decide
which one might resemble the son he and Doreen had always
wanted but never could conceive.

SOFT light of early evening still fought to keep darkness at bay
when he drove into the pebbled parking area alongside Tony
Fisheyes. He smiled at a grimy neon sign which flashed on as he
opened his van door. It read, "T O _ _ F I S H _ Y E S." Everyone
agreed the sign was much more appropriate without its burned-
out letters. Below the neon sign was a smaller hand-painted
sign with six bullet holes in it. It read, "NO MALE HUNTERS
ALLOWED." And below that an even smaller sign read, "Well-
behaved loggers tolerated—sometimes." Tony's blatant discrimi-
nations had never been successfully challenged.

Tony Fisheyes's exterior celebrated vintage early twentieth-
century ramshackle. Log and frame siding confessed to long-
term neglect by a painter's brush. A shake roof despaired of just
enough lost shakes to sprinkle Tony's customers on any day of
heavy rains. A missing middle step in stairs to the front door
tested the resolve of Tony's guests when they arrived and their
sobriety when they departed. Cracked and paint-stained front
windows displayed old dirty beer signs, some of which adver-
tised beers not brewed in more than twenty years. Like a drunken
eagle's nest, Tony's place of business clung in disarray to the top
of a granite promontory. Stubborn and unrelenting, it flaunted
its dilapidation and dared winter's shrieking winds to dislodge
it from its perch and send it to merciful interment in the river
below. The tavern's disreputable appearance encouraged most
anglers to spend their evenings and their money elsewhere. But
it suited most river guides and a few fishermen who preferred
anonymity and authenticity to prominence and façade.

Thirstier patrons stalled out at the front-room bar, which

provided only six stools for sitting. For visual pondering, barroom walls provided faded photographs and dusty wall mounts of vanquished trophy fish. Dozens of dead eyes glared their accusations around the room, scolding the sober and spooking the inebriated. Behind the bar, a ten-foot horizontal portrait of a reclining, well-endowed nude resting on one arm delivered equally provocative but more pleasant eye contact. To be sure they didn't go unnoticed, "No Smoking" signs rimmed the portrait. In a corner stood a stuffed pseudo-hunting trophy, a tribute to Tony's contempt for those who carried lethal weapons of animal destruction. A taxidermist's fanciful creation, the trophy was a fearsome, twice life-sized, man-altered, stuffed animal with a rabbit's body, big buck teeth, and two long pronged horns emerging from its head—a classic rendition of the mythical jackalope. A prominent bullet hole in the middle of the creature's forehead was ringed with telltale powder marks, giving it a disturbing three-eyed appearance.

Most dining patrons congregated in a small, poorly lit back room, which provided a dozen booths scattered around the sides and sized just right for six to crowd into space for four. In the center, one long community table accommodated ten—or more, for those unconcerned about confidentiality of their conversations and not so choosy about their evening company. When the weather cooperated, and sometimes even when it didn't, a crowd could assemble outside on a rickety and roofless redwood deck. Stained with tobacco juice and other foul substances, abused and scarred by logger's boots, the deck canted as it extended precariously out from the promontory and leaned over the river below. For squeamish patrons, bench seating was available along a protective railing missing only a few of its vital rails.

In a booth's intimacy, angling dinner guests talked intently about declining fortunes of the Klamath and its fish. While sitting around the long table or gathered on the deck, they traded wild stories about the Klamath and its fish or about other rivers and other fish. All stories were treated with respect or derision, depending not on accuracy and credibility of content but on telling skill and enthusiasm. "The guides' gaggle," Doreen called gatherings at Tony Fisheyes. "All noise and nonsense. There's more bologna served in there than Tony packs in his fishermen's lunches."

Drivers and loggers, a swaggering and rowdy bunch, clustered at Tony's too, mostly for ceremonious beer drinking. Single men came to avoid loneliness; married men came to avoid an evening of ritual bickering. In the twilight of long summer evenings, they wagered on beer bottle throws across the Klamath gorge. Losers were obliged to retrieve the litter by dawn's sober light, using a small dinghy Tony kept moored below his tavern for that purpose. Guides and rafters who traveled the river learned to avoid Tony's nightly beer bottle storms and cursed his patrons when they found short-toss strays floating downriver the next day. With an unintentional cruelty that sometimes accompanies good-natured rivalry, huskier competitors argued loudly about who could pitch Tommy Two Stumps furthest into the river. Tommy actually enjoyed their attention. He squealed in mock fear and begged the milder-mannered fishing guides to protect him.

After dark the beer drinkers staged a pissing contest—who could pee uninterrupted the longest. They drank until their gullets sloshed and held it until their bladders threatened to explode. Their eyes teared from the pain of delaying nature's urgent call for relief. Then they stood at the edge of the redwood deck, and, with beatific smiles of release, drenched the river below. King of the Klamath pissers was a grizzled, runty trucker named Peepee Simpson. His four minute, seventeen-second effort established the river record, until it was disqualified when his friends learned that he suffered from a mild enlargement of the prostate. Peepee continued to compete, but with a fifty-percent time reduction handicap to compensate for the unfair advantage of an impinged flow. He never regained his crown.

A new generation of timber workers now harvested the Klamath forests. Charlie didn't know many and he avoided them. Drivers and loggers from Charlie's era were mostly gone. They had moved elsewhere, to better opportunities or to the same jobs in different forests. Or they gave up and moved to the city when their nerves went bad or when they lost their strength to age, infirmity, or abuse. Or they died from accidents, abused livers, or fights with plantation workers.

A few contemporaries remained. Like Tommy Two Stumps, they wandered the Klamath in their nightly quest for companionship. They settled in at Tony Fisheyes or places like it scattered along the river. Most were mind-weary and maimed in body or in spirit. When they lost touch with reality, they spent their evenings absorbed in self-perpetuating melancholy, maudlin drunkenness, garrulous argument, and exaggerated complaint. Charlie avoided them too. "Flotsam and jetsam of the Klamath," Doreen called them. "The river's trash. It always washes ashore at the nearest bar." Charlie was appalled at these derelicts of the Klamath timber industry and the uselessness of their lives. He feared he soon might easily, too easily, follow a similar purposeless path into an itinerate and irresolute old age.

WITH his back to the door, the tavern's proprietor was washing glasses when Charlie entered, placing them carefully on shelves and overhead racks behind the bar. Without turning, Tony announced loudly, "Hey, everyone, the Hawk has landed." Several back-room patrons snickered. Charlie couldn't see them yet but he knew who was there: Tommy Two Stumps and others whom hope had abandoned. Perhaps Straw Hat Harry. Still too early for most fishing guides.

"Okay, Tony, how did you know?" Charlie challenged. "Even your fisheyes can't see behind you."

"Easy, Hawk. Easy. It's your natural Indian stealth. You're my only customer who never lets the door bang shut. When you come in you always catch it first."

"He's lyin', Hawk," Tommy Two Stumps shouted from the back room. "He's got a tiny mirror behind the bar, so no one can take him by surprise when his back is turned."

Tony turned around then. Quivering with laughter and

good humor, his great round belly was only partially covered by a stained white apron embroidered with a grotesque fish-head caricature. Tony was a living replica of his apron insignia. His bulbous eyes protruded unnaturally from their shallow sockets. They fixed on Charlie with a cold glare, a contradictory paradox to Tony's natural risibility. His lashless lids recessed far back into his skull. No one could recall ever seeing them blink, even when an occasional smoker temporarily evaded Tony's no smoking house rule and filled the tavern with smoke before Tony threw him out. Tony was nearly bald, and there was only indistinguishable blond fuzz where his eyebrows should have been. His hairlessness accentuated his fish-like stare. Pouchy bags of flesh beneath his eyes, a wide flat nose with flaring nostrils, puffed, crimson-flushed cheeks, beefy lips that curled back in a permanent pucker, and layer after layer of beard-stubbled wattles undulating from chin to shirt collar completed Tony's piscatorial facial features.

"Is he giving you the fisheye, Hawk?" Tommy called.

"Yeah," Charlie called back, as he returned Tony's glare. "But I'm giving him the Hawkeye."

The backroom patrons jumped from their seats, lifted Tommy Two Stumps, chair and all, and rushed into the front room, where they converged on the bar to watch the famous staredown. Recently retired from plantation work, with "indolence money" he called it, Straw Hat Harry was on the scene and encouraged Charlie. "Get him, Hawk. He's just a loathsome dead salmon waiting for some bird of prey to pluck his eyeballs."

"Naw," Charlie answered. "Dead salmon are for scavengers. This one's a stupid, lazy grouper growing fat and juicy behind his reef, just the target for a hungry shark. I'll give him the shark's eye." With menace etched into his features, Charlie leaned forward and the spectators cheered. He was one of only a few who, when sober, could tolerate Tony's fish-eyed glare indefinitely without dropping his gaze. "That's why his customers drink so much," Doreen once told Charlie. "They can't stand looking into those awful fisheyes without first numbing their senses.

They're afraid his eyes will read their secret thoughts and reveal their petty faults."

"But a grouper is still too much for a hawk." Tony continued to laugh with his perpetual good nature showing, even though he knew his customers welcomed a chance to side against him. "A bird like you, Hawk, has no place in the water. And you know there is terrible bad luck in a stare from old Tony Fisheyes."

Charlie shivered. Tony's comment touched an old Indian superstition. But Charlie's slate-colored eyes held firm and unyielding. "Enough of your fisheye, Tony. I'm hungry and you know I'm your best customer."

"Oldest customer, Hawk. Oldest. Not best. You don't drink enough any more. I can't get rich on one beer a night. Not even that when you're not working. What happened to your thirst?"

"I'm saving it, Tony. For our old age. You know I'm your annuity. I've got injun guts, and I'll survive long after you've poisoned all your other customers with bad food, stale beer, and grouper breath."

Tony spread his massive hands on the bar top and heaved his great bulk forward against the bar until only a few inches separated the intent faces of the two stare-down combatants. The added pressure on his bloated innards was too much, and Tony unleashed a lingering, sonorous belch. Charlie didn't flinch.

"*Aggh*...grouper breath. Smell the corruption." Straw Hat Harry covered his nose and mouth with his hand. Everyone else booed and moved back a step.

The pressure still wasn't relieved, and Tony lifted his left leg. "Look out Hawk, he's gonna fart," someone in the crowd roared.

Tony forced a grim smile of defiance, flexed his abdominal muscles, and broke wind. His flatulence was gale force and bass resonant. Sound waves rattled glasses on the shelves behind him. Charlie still didn't flinch. The crowd booed again and retreated further.

Tony belched once more. "I eat my own food, Hawk. Every day. I drink my own beer, and—"

"Yeah. More'n anybody," Tommy Two Stumps interrupted and clapped his hands in glee.

Tony tried to continue. "—and I'm doing fine, and—"

"If you call three hundred and thirty pounds fine," Tommy interrupted again.

"It's because you've got grouper's guts," Charlie snarled. "Your system processes anything and extracts every gram of nourishment from it. Hell, Tony, you could get fat eating rotten fish and drinking loggers' piss—"

"Which is what your food and beer taste like," Tommy chimed in. The spectators all cheered again.

The entire bar shook with varied reverberations from Tony's laughter-convulsed body. Tears drained down his face. His eyes remained unblinking, but he dropped his glare. "All right, Hawk. You win—this time. Go sit down. I'll bring your piddly, solo beer and tell the kitchen to prepare your last supper."

Charlie followed the crowd returning Tommy Two Stumps to his station of prominence in the back room. Tommy was animated and waived Charlie over. "You got him, Hawk. You got him." Tommy pummeled Charlie about the forearms with his chubby little fists.

Charlie didn't smile. He towered over Tommy, and his tepee hat shadowed most of the table like a giant sombrero. "I need to ask you something, Tommy."

"Sure, Hawk, sure." Tommy fidgeted under Charlie's glare.

"You talk to a stranger about me a month ago?"

"No...no, Hawk. I wouldn't...I wouldn't do that."

"You sure? A fisherman, maybe from San Francisco?" Charlie intensified his glare and let Tommy squirm.

"No...uh...wait a minute. I remember." Tommy swallowed uncomfortably, and his sallow complexion turned crimson as he blushed. "There was a guy here. Real friendly. Looking for a fishing guide. I told him you were the best."

"And a few other things too?"

"Well, maybe. I can't remember."

"Like my working in the growers' camps?"

"I reckon I did. Hell, Hawk, it ain't no secret. Like I said, he seemed real friendly. But I didn't tell him about your...uh, your bad luck guiding, Hawk. I didn't tell him nothin' about that." Tommy was sweating. "Is it okay, Hawk? Tell me it ain't no problem. I swear I didn't say nothin' about your bad luck."

"It's okay, Tommy." Charlie felt genuine compassion and affection for the legless little man he'd crippled for life. "Thanks for your recommend. Next beer's on me."

Tommy sighed with relief.

Charlie massaged his neck to relieve tension from the staredown and walked to a vacant booth. The right of a solo customer to privacy in one of Tony's booths was generally respected. Tony's patrons were used to Charlie's moodiness and left him alone when he obviously wanted to be alone. He searched the crowd for Straw Hat Harry, caught his friend's eye, and called him over. "Tell me what's going on at the plantations, Harry. I'm out of touch."

"Mostly confusion, Hawk." Harry brought his beer, sat down opposite Charlie and tweaked but didn't remove his hat, which was one size too small and perched high above his ears. Never without his trademark, Harry treated himself to a new straw hat every two years. Biennially, Harry's head topping changed color, but never style. Hat styles changed, but Harry's straw hats never did. He wore the same uniformly-brimmed, fedora-type, Panama hat. Harry's hat vintage was readily ascertainable from the degree of grime build-up along its turned-down front rim, which Harry fingered nervously when he talked. His hat stayed on Harry all seasons. He claimed it protected his fair complexion from all ravages of sun and light. It also roosted on top of Harry day and night. He insisted it warmed his hairless scalp. As protection, his hat was only a partial success, for Harry's long aquiline nose protruded well beyond the protection zone and remained red throughout the year, shading darker to a deep color of pickled beets in summer, and fading to a mottled roseate, webbed with tiny, purple spider veins in winter.

Although few ever saw the top of Harry's head, his wife Rosie confirmed that it was indeed there and that it was in fact hairless. She also confided to Doreen that Harry, because he thought he was so sensitive to open-window drafts in summer and cold-room drafts in winter, even wore his hat to bed, where it could be dislodged only by unusual exertions during infrequent amorous episodes—or by Rosie, when she cautiously removed it after Harry fell asleep, replacing it carefully at dawn before he awoke. Despite its apparent perpetual constriction, an agile and crafty mind thrived beneath the hat. Harry remained the only contemporary friend whose company Charlie still genuinely enjoyed.

Harry leaned forward and adopted a conspiratorial posture. "There's a lot of confusion in the camps," he said. "We're both fortunate to be out of it. God, Hawk, you're not thinking of going back?"

"No. I'm out for good. I promised Doreen...and myself."

"The growers will take you back, Hawk. They need help with their drying sheds. They're burning each other out, and they're doing it the smart way, burning sheds instead of fields. Tempers are hot, too. There'll be a lot of killing in the future if the burning doesn't stop. From what I hear about your not catching fish, I think you should—"

"Aye, and if this isn't a two-hat conspiracy," Willie McPherson's booming brogue interrupted them as he approached the booth from the barroom. "Hawk, yer mickle ten-gallon black wigwam be nigh to devour that poor anemic sunbonnet on top o' Harry. The two o' ye be brim to brim in mysterious conversations." In the middle of the table, Willie deposited a bedraggled green and blue plaid tam ornamented with a new pompom of black yarn. Then he gripped Charlie on the shoulder and slid into the booth next to Harry. His ruddy features beamed with good humor. His eyes, locked in the perpetual squint of an alert river guide, darted merrily back and forth between his two friends.

"Nothing mysterious about fishing, Willie," Harry responded, "except figuring out how the Hawk can catch one."

"Aye, and it's not the fishin' ye be palaverin' about this night. The looks of ye be far too dern, too gloomy and serious fer that."

"It's serious enough." Charlie looked glum. "I'm twenty-nine days now without a good fish."

"Aye, Charlee, ye sur be feelin' the bain, the curse o' the Klamath this year. So luck passed ye by again today?"

"Not much luck today. Only half-pounders."

"It's gettin' bad…wanchancy fer all o' us, Hawk." Willie ran a hand through his wild, bristling, and kinky thatch of unruly red hair. "The steelhead count, even the wee little quarter kilos, be down fer all us poor overworked, underpaid, underfed, underappreciated, and underfermented guides. There be far too few gude fish in the river."

"We can only take what the river gives us," Charlie said with resignation in his voice. "The philosophy of my ancestors."

"More Indian nonsense," Harry scoffed. "Presenting the obvious as some great tribal wisdom. There'd be a lot more steelhead for upriver fishermen, if coastal Indian tribes didn't harvest so many fish coming into the Klamath."

Charlie was sensitive to contentious arguments that pitted Indian fishing rights against sport-fishing interests. He avoided participation in that controversy, because he couldn't resolve the same conflicts that warred about in his own mind.

"Aye, and it's costin' us fishermen," Willie said. "We be losin' a lot o' fishermen. They always be seekin' new rivers fer more trout and fer the big brag. Always chasin' the big brag, they are. They be flockin' north now, like geese fly south in fall. Each year more and more quit the Klamath and go north where steelhead be larger and more plentiful. And there be precious few new starters comin' here to replace the quitters. I be thinkin' this be me last Klamath season. Time fer Wanderin' Willie to wander north too. I be goin' to Canady next year."

"The timber harvest is also winding down," Harry said and tugged at his hat. "I've been listening to the loggers here at night. They're all worried. The timber companies are still racing through the forests. Most of them, even older companies, harvest far in excess of new growth replacement. They're shipping like crazy to Japan and other far-east customers, straight out of the port at Eureka. Everyone was busy last year, and there was a lot of money flowing on the Klamath. But it can't last much longer. The loggers think it's slowing down already. Some companies have already cut back their crews. Owl lovers won the environmental war, and most companies are accelerating their current contracts, shipping as much as possible, because they know they soon will have to curtail or even terminate cutting in the Klamath and many other forests. When that happens, and many loggers say it's started already, the Klamath will be filled with loggers and truckers out of work who have no place to go. The problem's aggravated because years of excess harvest have brought in a lot of excess people. Our river economy has been over-stimulated on a temporary basis."

Harry paused to finish his beer and waive his hand request for another. Then he continued, "When logging companies are finally forced out, our Klamath communities and businesses will die, like mining towns that died almost overnight after the gold rush ended. The river will still flow, but its economy will run dry. There's nothing coming to replace logging. The river draws more and more rafters, but they don't spend money here. They provision elsewhere, and they use the river's campgrounds instead of our motels and lodges. The marijuana plantations can't last much longer either. The Feds must be getting closer to a major bust."

Willie chimed in. "Aye, and it's sure a river o' lost souls ye soon be livin' on, Hawk, a river o' lost souls. It's naught but a fey future fer the Klamath and those who stay here. There be no siller, no money on the Klamath. The fishin' be gone. The minin' be gone. The loggin' be gone. Even the smoker growin' be gone. And nothin' be left but lost souls with nowhere to go." Willie paused, looked first at Charlie and then at Harry, smiled, and then laughed. "But this be right now, old Charlee the Hawker, and right now there be ye and there be me, and there be old Harry here with his sissy hat. And we fer sure don't be lost yet. And right now I got to take care o' me turrible thirst. I need me daily measure o' the Chivas. It be the elixir of life to any Scot.

And the deprivation of it, even fer only a day, be a inhuman torture o' the spirit no true Scot can abide." Willie turned his head toward the barroom. "Tony," he yelled into the other room, "ye dowf, ye fule, ye loon, ye great round mound o' blubber topped with codfish eyes, where be me stoup o' the amber nectar? Aye, and ye better bring me two."

Tony waddled to the table. His pudgy hands encircled three juice glasses filled to the brim. He banged them down on the table without spilling a drop. "Here, you besotted son of besotted parentage descended from besotted ancestors of a besotted nation. Here's your full ration. Don't bother me no more tonight."

"Aye. Thankee Tony. But, ye shilpit, ye great bloat bag o' foul wind and internal corruptions, ye unjustly malign me ancestry. It be the depraved Irish, not the cautious Scots, who be the enemies o' temperance. We Scots imbibe no more than sobriety's natural limit. A full mutchkin. No more, no less. We be far too frugal to waste our pennies on any excess drams."

"Scot. Irish. You're both the obnoxious same, spouting words no one understands." Tony harrumphed and waddled off.

"Aye. And our thirst be a undeserved blessin' to all ye doited tavern owners," Willie shouted after him.

Willie drained his first glass in one long draught. He leaned back, closed his eyes and smiled. "Aye, that be gude. That be so-o-o gude. That be the purest remedy for all me ills. It fires me dampened spirit, rests me poor tired body, polishes me river-rusted brain, and liberates me fettered voice. Now, be we havin' some more o' these serious conversations or do I regale ye with the lyrical beauty o' me favored songs?"

Harry grimaced. "We talk now. You can sing later."

"Aye, more talk it is then." Willie opened his eyes. "What about the fish, Hawk? Yer been orful quiet this evenin'. Be they returnin'...the fish?"

Charlie's expression was impassive, his voice subdued. "Someday."

"Even the big runs like when we were boys?" Harry asked.

"Someday."

"When the fish-killing ends?"

"Yes."

Willie scoffed. "The fish-killin' end? It'll ne'er end."

"It will end. Someday."

"How, Hawk?"

"There'll be a no-kill regulation."

"Even for Indians?"

Charlie sighed. "Even for Indians."

"Ne'er, Hawk. Fish-killers be too vocal."

"They're in the minority now and fewer each year."

"Aye. They be fewer and fewer. But like all wee people who think their rights be getting' squeezed, they be louder and louder with the protestin'."

"He's right, Hawk," Harry said. "Regulators listen to noise, not reason."

"They can't forever. I'll wait."

"You don't have forever, Hawk."

"The river does. I'll still wait."

"So ye be stayin' on the river then, Hawk?" Willie began sipping from his second glass.

"Yes."

"Even if the fishin' be gone?"

"Yes."

"Get off the river Hawk," Harry said. "Before you end up a tavern dweller like me and Tommy Two Stumps...and others like us. The day of the fisherman and the logger...and even the grower...is over. Like the fur-trapper, the hunter and the prospector before them. This time there's nothing to replace what we do. The river will die."

"Not the river, Harry." Charlie seemed to look beyond his two friends. "Maybe its small towns. But not the river. The river never dies. Its fish decline, but they will replenish. Its forests are stripped, but new trees will grow. We've all abused, exploited, or neglected the Klamath in some way, but it will survive. When towns die, people leave. Maybe that's a good thing. Clear the river's valleys and forests of people and their century-and-a-half of litter, and give the Klamath time to heal its wounds. It will, if we give it a chance."

"Aye, Hawk, but will we?" Willie was skeptical. "A river be a powerful seductress, nature's own people magnet. Maybe land sellers be next. From San Francisco they be comin'. To buy, subdivide, and sell. Ye stay here, Hawk, and ye fer sure be golfin' on the Klamath in yer old age. Land sellers soon be buildin' houses up and down the whole Klamath strath. I can see signs all along Highway 96, 'River Homes Fer Sale'. Maybe city people be tired o' cities. Maybe they be wantin' river homes. Then they be needin' their fancy restaurants, their fancy shops and their fancy golf courses. Then the old Hawker, he be playin' golf instead o' fishin'." Willie laughed and pounded his fist on the table. "Poor Charle-e-e. He be stayin' here to avoid the cities, but the cities be comin' to him."

"Not in our lifetime, Hawk...nor in yours, Willie," Harry said. "The Klamath is too remote. Urbanize the Klamath? It can't happen."

"Aye, Harry. Maybe so, maybe not. I be goin' north so I won't be here to see. Why do ye stay, Hawk, and bide the bent, if the cities they be chasin' ye?"

"I can't leave. I don't know anything else."

"You're smart, Hawk, smarter than most," Harry said. "You could find work in the city, join Doreen in Eureka."

Charlie shook his head. "I can't. I can't work anywhere with only four walls around me...and a window if I was lucky. Endure the tiresome chatter of city people all day long? It would drive me crazy. I need to stay here for a lot of reasons that are important to me, reasons others may not understand."

Harry tweaked his hat impatiently. "What's so important, Hawk, that you risk becoming another local derelict, a used-up has-been that summer tourists point out to their children? 'See, Johnny, there's a toothless old Indian with a funny hat, dozing in the sunshine! Ask him if we can take his picture.'"

Again, Charlie's expression grew dreamy and detached. "It's not easy to explain. I need to live by the river for the freedom of my spirit. I always have. I need to die by the river for the immortality of my soul, like others need food for the mortality of their bodies. For sense of value and strength of purpose, I need to hear and see all the sounds and sights of the river and its people, even the crazy ones. For comfort, I need to know that the river spirits of my Hupok ancestors are near. For contentment, I need to stay connected with my Indian heritage, even with its frailty, uncertainty, and superstition. All these things I need, though they cause me to suffer the intolerance of others, though I become impoverished to keep them, and even though they deny me companionship of my only other love."

"Aye, Hawk," Willie's voice softened and became more subdued. "Ye fer sure be stoor, uncommon stubborn. What about yer dark-haired, dark-eyed lass?"

Charlie paused a moment. There was sadness in his eyes. "Yes, I need Doreen. For all the other longings of my heart, I need her. But...don't you see?...I have her. I have her love. I know that. The burning blood of youth has cooled, and I don't need to be with her every day. Nor Doreen with me. Not now. Not after all these years. She's as secure in her knowledge of my love for her. Sure she needs me. But she needs me as I am, not as I never can be. She prefers a weekly phone call and occasional visit with a wild and free Hupok savage to the daily presence of an urbanized and miserable Indian misfit. For her depth of understanding I'm richly blessed. She knows I'll never leave the river, and she accepts that. She's happy by the sea.

"It's like the no-return commitment of drift boats floating on the Klamath. Once they're on the river, they have to keep going. They can't turn back. Like a drift boat, my life is consigned to the Klamath. I'm captive to it, and I can't turn back. I think I knew that even when I was a small boy and searched in vain for Tawahana, the river's source. The bond that keeps me here is still as strong as it was in childhood and still as difficult for me to explain."

"So, yer mind be fixed, then. Ye stay, like some old gray Klamath monolith?"

"Yes. The river's fate is my fate, my destiny." Charlie's voice had a ring of finality to it.

"And mine," Harry said. "I'll never leave either."

"Aye. Tony can ill afford your absence."

All three were silent then. Charlie seemed to withdraw into a private world where others could not follow. Sensing their friend's mood had turned introspective and exclusionary, Wandering Willie and Straw Hat Harry left Charlie's booth to join the gathering at the community table, now unusually quiet.

Charlie dined alone with his thoughts. He still had a tough decision to make.

JOY AND SORROW

CHARLIE LEFT TONY FISHEYES as confused and un-decided as when he'd entered. Darkness settled in, and he drove home surrounded by the stygian gloom that rivers gather about them. He shivered as night-chill, his only companion, crowded into the truck with him. The chill seemed to penetrate his clothing and his skin, as if night spirits were conspiring to add physical discomfort to his mental torment. *It's too early...they shouldn't even be out yet.*

Grumbling, he exited his van. Approaching his doorstep, he mispositioned his feet, stumbled, and nearly fell *Three nights ago. the unnatural absence of light was my friend and it protected me. Now it's my enemy and it betrays me...or am I losing so much balance that I grow clumsy on dry land too...or does it now take only one beer to unsteady me?* He'd forgotten to leave a light on, and his cabin was tenebrous, silent, and uninviting. He hesitated before entering, as if uncertainty held his body as well as his mind captive.

Solemn sounds from a nearby tree greeted him, and he listened intently. There it was again. Brief high-pitched hoots with evenly spaced intervals between, like the barking of a small dog, progressed to a longer series of rapid hoots in a growing crescendo. An answering call echoed back from the gorge below. *No...oh yes it is...*he nodded his head...*the hunting cry of the spotted owl...Siiko, old dark eyes himself. I knew I saw a pair of black eyes...not yellow like other owls...staring at me at dusk last week.*

Driven out of the high mountains by loggers. Probably a young pair whose ancestral nesting trees were harvested, so they've come back here to the Klamath gorge. How ironic. The bird that alters destiny for this generation of loggers...and maybe for all the Klamath... finds sanctuary among old-growth remnants in my own back yard. To console me and make evenings of my old age less lonely? What my father didn't think possible may happen, and the cause of birds and fishes may yet prevail over the commercial needs of a modern society.

If logging has to leave the Klamath forests, as Straw Hat Harry thinks, then someday my grandsons may see the Klamath as I did fifty years ago. When they come next June, I must tell them.

The owls repeated their hunting calls and then were silent. A flapping and whoosh of wings announced the closer bird's departure. Total darkness conceded to a hint of moonlight. *Clouds breaking up?* But the air felt muggy, and he frowned and looked up. Like a delicate gauze curtain, a veil of haze spread across the sky and extended to the moonsliver whose rising tip pierced the eastern horizon. *Rain tomorrow? Should improve the fishing. If I reject Alden's offer, maybe I'll spend a day alone on the river...and not fish. Yes, even in the rain that would be nice...to float the river for pleasure, enjoy the surroundings, and not have to accommodate others, not be responsible for their safety as well as their success...and to reassure the Klamath that I don't seek to exploit it.*

Once inside his home, habit took over, and he went to his fly-tying desk in the back bedroom. Unlike his sometimes uncooperative legs, his hands hadn't lost any of their agility. Working swiftly, he tied a half-dozen skunk patterns on size four hooks. Like a gifted composer at the piano, his big hands flew about the vise, executing delicate finger maneuvers flawlessly, seeming without effort. He smiled at a memory of his family watching the process.

———

DOREEN STANDS BEHIND HIM with her hands resting on his shoulders, her fingers working, digging deep to massage stiffness out of his neck and shoulder muscles. "You have a surgeon's hands," she whispers. "How I love to watch you tie. Your skill and speed fascinate me." His restless young daughters refuse to linger. They stay briefly and then giggle in unison, "How boring, Dad," as they flee the room.

———

SOON FINISHED, CHARLIE inspected the results of his efforts. Dissatisfied with the drab appearance of a standard skunk pattern, Charlie frowned, returned the flies to his vise and added three wraps of florescent green chenille to the shank of each fly. *It's a better rain pattern for tomorrow,* as if tomorrow's decision was finally made. *I prefer a skunk with a green butt...but who knows about a steelhead.* He shrugged his shoulders.

Feeling restless, he paced through the cabin, paused at a bookshelf, and absently scanned its titles. He knew he wouldn't be able to concentrate enough to read, not now. *Should I call Doreen?...more damn indecision.* He resumed pacing, then stopped at a window, stared out at the sky, and watched clouds with silvered linings slide across the moonsliver. No answers there, either. He shrugged his shoulders again and winced when he felt pain growing deep beneath his shoulder blades. He reached back and tried unsuccessfully to dig his fingers into the source of his ache. *Where are her fingers when I need them?* He finally sat down at the telephone and dialed Doreen.

Doreen was surprised but pleased with his unexpected call. She sympathized with his lack of fishing success and his client's poor skill and attitude. He didn't tell her about the incident at Dragon's Tooth Rapids. He did tell her about Alden's offer.

"What did you say to him?" she asked.

"I told him I'd think about it."

"When do you have to decide?"

"Tonight. So I can give him an answer tomorrow."

"Have you decided?"

"No. Not yet."

"Have you thought about it?"

"All evening."

"I'm glad you're talking to me before you decide."

"I'm glad too." He felt some of the tension drain from his body.

"And I'm also glad you haven't asked me what I think you should do."

"I'm not ready to ask you. And I may not ask you. I have to decide."

"That's what I think too. But I'm still glad you talked to me first."

He was silent a moment. She didn't interrupt his silence. "Doreen?" he asked.

"Yes, Charlie?"

"I've thought about a lot of things."

"What things?" She was patient.

"I told Alden this afternoon that the Klamath has always been my joy and my sorrow. I wasn't sure what I meant then, but I think I know now."

"Tell me, Charlie the Hawk. Tell me about your joy and sorrow."

He paused, then he spoke softly in the intimate, storytelling voice she knew so well. "I looked deep into the Siskiyou Mountains three times and saw three separate visions, each representing a different stage of my life and a different gift from the Klamath, each with its own mixture of joy and sorrow." He paused to clear his throat and continued, "In my first vision I saw the Siskiyous as a small boy, half a century ago. I saw high forests still uncut, silent, and full of mystery and half-remembered Indian legends. When I was old enough, my father took me there. For two summers we searched for the lost river of gold. Of course we didn't find it. The few grains and occasional nugget we did find barely covered the cost of our provisions.

"My father was a kind but silent man who rarely spoke except to answer questions. It was like we were together but alone together...if that makes any sense. But I did learn all my father could tell and show me about his native tribe, which wasn't very much. He was one of fewer than a hundred remaining pure-blooded Hupoks; there may be none now. He told me about his tribe's primitive stone weapons, their obsession with wealth, and their unusual esteem for women. Unlike other Klamath tribes, the Hupoks had no medicine men. Their doctors were all women, and the Hupoks were the only Klamath tribe who didn't kill doctors who couldn't effect a cure.

"I learned from my father how to survive in the wilderness, perhaps as only an Indian knows, and I learned that rare feeling of peace that comes when you truly master solitude. Despite all I learned from my father, I didn't feel close to my father, not even during those two summers. He didn't show feelings or emotions...even to me. He seemed too preoccupied with our search for gold, making sure we had food, and clearing our campsites of purple scorpions. I never saw joy in my father's face. I never heard anger or frustration in his voice. I don't know if he felt those emotions, and I never felt part of him. I accompanied my father but I was never with my father. He didn't teach me closeness, because he couldn't teach me what he didn't know. I wonder if closeness of mind and spirit, that nonphysical feeling of intimacy that binds one person to another, was something missing in my Hupok ancestors."

"Do you fear that it's also missing in you?" she asked gently.

"Sometimes."

"With me?" Her heart skipped a beat, and she felt a sudden blood rush of anxiety—for him, not for herself.

"Never with you. Sometimes with others."

She smiled and her anxiety subsided. "So, your mixed blood produces mixed results?"

He sighed. "Something like that. Through my mother I feel bound to you, emotionally as well as physically. Through my father I feel bound to the earth, sky, and water, but with something missing. Something is incomplete. When I was very young, my father told me a lot about the Klamath. In Indian terms, he described the two different sources that provide the river's fury and its peace. He promised to take me there, but he never did. And then the magical years of childhood were gone, and it was too late to renew a father's forgotten promise. I've never been to where the river begins. I think I'm afraid to go now, because I know I won't find there either what my father described or what I once imagined.

"So, the Klamath's first gift was my Hupok heritage with its Indian knowledge and imagery, but also with its impassivity, detachment, and lack of reality. This was the joy and sorrow of my youth."

He paused again. She was silent and let him gather his thoughts. Then he continued. "The second time I looked to the horizon as a young man. I saw the Siskiyous as they were when I was the best at driving logging trucks. Worked-over forest sections lay silent, naked, and bleeding, gashed to their mantles by clear-cutting. Above them was fresh activity, and those forest sections were vibrant, busy, and full of life, hope, and achievement. Then I saw you, young and radiant in your hand-sewn peasant blouse, as you were when we first met, harvesting apple orchards in the Seiad Valley. Confined by a red kerchief, your long raven's hair was all knotted on top of your head, except for one loose strand that trailed out behind you, streaming in the wind. You kept batting at it with your hand, and you were sunburned, carefree, and laughing...and full of happiness and mischief.

"Then I saw us picnicking with Michele and Carleen. We rested in splotches of sunshine among the leopard lilies, trilliums, wild iris, and ginger blooming in a green meadow that embraces the headwaters of Indian Creek. Our daughters ran barefoot through the stream, chasing schools of trout, splashing each other, and squealing at contact with icy cold water. The only tracks in the sand beside Indian Creek were from their tiny feet and a pair of elk who had stopped earlier to drink.

"But failure and tragedy marred that vision. It was impure and tormented...tormented by my loss of driving nerve, by my terrible accidents, and the shame that followed, by the shame of two years in the growers' camps...years that were a betrayal of you and our daughters, and, yes, even a betrayal of myself to satisfy those stupid needs that keep me forever bound to the

Klamath. And the worst torment of all, the wound that never heals: Carleen's addiction to that awful drug I helped supply, the one so many say is harmless but eventually caused her death.

"So the Klamath's second gift was pride of manhood, a good livelihood on the river and, most precious of all, the blessings of love and a family. But for all the river gave, it also took back. It took my pride and replaced it with shame. The noxious product of its forests took the life of our last born, and now the Klamath reduces my livelihood to almost nothing. I worry if the river will someday destroy us as well. This is the joy and sorrow of my years as a young man…and—"

"You leave something out, Charlie," she interrupted, looking at the photographs she kept beside the telephone. The faces of the man she knew so well smiled hauntingly at her. "You leave out something the Klamath hasn't taken back."

"What's that?"

"You leave out courage. That's never been taken from you. You've always had the strength to overcome adversity and try again. You've never given up, like so many, like those relics from the past in Tony Fisheyes. You've made mistakes, but you've always tried, and the river continues to forgive you. The Klamath tests you and you always respond. You've never given in to disappointment or despair. You've been desolated, but never defeated." She paused and laughed, "Think about it, Charlie, even old Tony Fisheyes can't stare you down."

He laughed then too. "Yes, the river has left me courage. For it leaves me you to remind me when I forget and to encourage me when I have doubts. For that I'm forever grateful."

"The third vision, Charlie? You looked into the mountains three times," she reminded him. "What did you see the third time?"

"The third time I looked to the Siskiyous I saw them through the eyes of an old man, and I felt serenity. I saw the Klamath of the future, a place of veneration…no longer exploited. I saw a safe home for all wild things, a haven where I could once again seek unspoiled headwaters in solitude...as I did when I was a small boy. But then that vision too became clouded.

"Now I grow closer to old age. My body wears out and no longer follows directions from my mind. My legs aren't strong enough to wade the river as it should be waded. The pain in my shoulders brings me a new weakness at the oars. Today, for the first time, I felt a failure of strength. It frightened me. I know I have some guiding days left on the river. But I don't know how many. I think not very many. The river denies me fish, and I think that must be a sign. My savings are low, but I still believe I must resist moving to Eureka or somewhere else.

"Alden's offer helps provide enough money to keep me on the river a few more years. If I go back into the mountains now, one more time, I think his money...always the goddam money... will be the key to joy in my old age. But I wonder...what will be my sorrow? That vision isn't clear. I think about it, and I'm afraid."

"Joy is seldom found in money, Charlie," she challenged. "Maybe the joy of your old age will come from something else and become a joy that doesn't bring sorrow."

"Maybe. But what else?"

"I don't know. You'll have to find out for yourself. I only know you can't appreciate joy if you don't know sorrow. So maybe sorrow comes first. Even the harshest of your Indian gods should be satisfied that you have too long born a burden of sorrow."

Again he felt his spirits lift. "Perhaps you're right. I'll have to think about it that way."

"What about Alden and his offer? Can you trust him?"

"I don't know. I don't think so."

"Why not?"

"It's instinctive. I've had negative signals since I first saw him, not strong signals but persistent and nagging. He's intelligent but he's too impatient. He's driven by ambition, and he seems callous and indifferent to others. I suspect he's ruthless and arrogant. He has no respect for the river."

"He also sounds glib and deceitful," she cautioned. "Ten thousand dollars is too much money just to help him gather material for a feature story. How do you know he is what he says he is?"

"I guess I don't know. He didn't show identification. I didn't think of asking."

"Did he mention anything he's written?"

"No."

"Or who he works for?"

"He said he's freelance."

"Charlie, maybe he really is part of a drug syndicate, or rival growers...or even one of the Mexican cartels."

"Maybe. I just don't know."

"Won't it be risky for you to show him the plantations?"

"Yes."

"And worse if this Alden is some kind of threat to them?"

"Yes, I've thought about that."

"Particularly if the growers suspect you're the one burning them out?" Her question was cautious.

His head jerked up, and he almost dropped the phone. "You know?"

"Of course."

"How?"

"I've always known. Since the first reports in summer. You're the only one who could do it. Even though you don't talk about it very often, I know how you feel about Carleen."

"I didn't want to endanger you. I thought you'd be safer if you didn't know."

"Does anyone else know?"

"No. No one."

"Won't the growers suspect you if you continue?"

"I don't think so. It wouldn't occur to them that the man who built their drying sheds would come back and burn them."

"And the forest you love so much? Doesn't your burning threaten them?"

"Not really. As a safety precaution when I built the sheds,

I made sure all undergrowth was cleared for a hundred yards around them."

She sighed. "When does it end, Charlie?"

"It's very simple. When the growers are gone, or when I'm dead."

"Don't they rebuild?"

"Yes. But not as quickly. The growers accuse each other, and Harry thinks they've started fighting each other. They may drive themselves out."

"My God, Charlie. You're starting a civil war among the growers?"

"Goddam right."

"But innocent people, like field workers, will get hurt."

"I know that. Wars always hurt the innocent."

"Doesn't that bother you?"

"Sure it bothers me."

"But you're going to continue anyway?"

"Yes. The government won't do anything to stop them."

"Please, Charlie. Please be careful."

"I am. I travel on foot and only during the new moon. I move with all the cunning of my ancestors...and with their fear, for they believed Owandaga, the night of the sleeping moon, released evil spirits to stalk the land. I leave the high benches quickly, before the fire begins to blaze, and I don't rest until I reach the valley. Only then do I feel safe, and I look back to see if there's an orange glow in the western sky, like a second sun setting, which tells me another drying shed has been destroyed. Then my fear is gone, for it's only a small fear...a genetic fear of darkest night, and not a fear of what I do. Afterward I'm tired, very tired. But the monster which is the anger in my soul has been fed and is once again at rest.

"And I'm also very careful because I think about you and what it might mean for you if some night I go into the mountains and don't return." His voice grew hesitant. "What will you do, Doreen...if once I don't return?"

She was silent a moment. Then she spoke softly. He could

barely hear her. "I know I will miss you very much. At first I will grieve, but I think it will be a quiet grief. I won't be able to cry. Not yet. I'll tell myself that you found in death what you somehow lost in life...pride...pride and peace...and I'll try not to be too sad. Then I will come back to the Klamath and fly the flag from your drift boat high above our cabin, with the hawk's head pointing proudly to the heavens for all to see...to see the Hawk is free and soaring in the sky. Then I'll sit by myself on our doorstep where we once sat together long ago. And then...finally...I will cry. I'll cry for a long time, for a very long time. Until I've finished mourning, finished all the mourning...for you and your shattered dreams, for Carleen and her shattered life, and for all you and I enjoyed together in youth but lost when our hair began to gray.

"When I'm done with mourning, I'll wipe away my tears. Then I'll remember other things, and I will rejoice. I'll rejoice for you and your unwavering devotion to a river, for Michele and Carleen and their unwavering devotion to each other, and for all you and I enjoyed together in youth and didn't lose when our hair began to gray. And then I'll go inside and throw out all your smelly long underwear and all your other awful fish clothes, except for your wonderful tepee hat which I'll save and mount outside for birds to make a nest in, so that other feathered creatures can share in a legacy from the Hawk."

Charlie laughed. "I like your plan," he said. Then he looked at a picture of his two grandsons beside his phone. "Would you do one more thing?"

"What is it, Charlie?"

"Take our grandsons to Tawahana, where the river begins, particularly to Wateela, the river's peace. I want their eyes to swell with wonder when they look upon the gardens of the Gods. I want fragrance from a million blossoms to intoxicate them. I want voices of a hundred different birds singing together to fill their heads with choral rapture. I want them thusly prepared, so, if they listen very carefully, they will hear the Gods laughing at play and clap their hands in delight."

"So many wants, Charlie. This sounds like a pilgrimage…and one you need to make."

"I know. I've thought about it. I'll ask Michele if I can take her sons in June when school is out. But, in case I can't, will you?"

"Yes, Charlie, I'll take them. But they are only small boys and may not experience the gardens as you so desperately wish them to. They may be indifferent, even bored."

"I know. But they are still young enough to see with their hearts. Who knows, they may even see Omahs and the unicorns and dinosaurs I once saw there…in my dreams. So they will know what to expect, I'll tell them about the river's beginnings, as I promised my father when I was a boy. But, if I cannot, you will have to."

"I will, Tamiko. I know the story. And I'll try to tell them as you would have done." Doreen fought to hold back her tears. "Now you have a choice to make. Choose carefully, Hawk, and listen to your heart. Let it tell you what to do. But if you decide to go back into the mountains, don't call me until you have done with it. I want to think of you safely drifting on the river you love so beyond reason, not sneaking about the plantations helping a man you don't trust do his dirty work."

Their goodbyes were brief and unemotional but full of unspoken concern for each other.

FROM his motel room on the outskirts of Happy Camp, Alden was also engrossed in a telephone conversation—with a man in San Francisco.

"Has he agreed?" the man asked.

"Not yet," Alden responded. "I asked him to think about it. He'll let me know tomorrow."

"Did he accept your story about being a feature writer?"

"I think so. He doesn't like me, but he asked a lot of questions and seemed satisfied with my answers."

"Be careful. Charlie the Hawk is no dummy. We've done some more checking. He could do a lot better for himself but won't leave the river. He's mostly self-educated, but he's an intelligent man, very intelligent."

"I'm not surprised. Those damned eyes of his seem to read my thoughts. He's not easily deceived."

"What if he turns you down? Is there another who could guide you?"

"No. The Hawk is the only one. If he refuses, I'll tell him who I really am and increase our offer."

"Alden, do you realize that puts this man's life in jeopardy?"

"I know. But I'll have no choice. It's the only way."

"What if you pressure up the daughter thing? I've seen the accident report. It's a classic. Young woman driving under the influence of mega-marijuana smokes. Talking nonstop…babbling nonsense according to the one non-smoker in the car… waving her hands aggressively. Lost in that typical drug-induced euphoria and immersed in her delusions of insightful brilliance, she simply missed a sharp turn, ran straight off the road head-on into a tree. Although she was killed instantly, none of the other five occupants had serious injuries."

Alden thought for a moment and frowned into the phone. "I don't like manipulating him that way." Then he sighed. "But I'll use it again if I think I have to."

"Okay…your call. Can you trust him with knowledge of your true identity?"

"Yes. I'm sure of it. It's a funny thing. I know The Hawk doesn't trust me, but I sense he's a most unusual and dedicated man, a man I can trust."

"His knowledge puts your life in jeopardy too."

"I know. But the stakes are high enough. I'll risk it." Alden spoke not with bravado but with calculating intensity.

"Okay. Good luck."

"Thanks. I'll need it."

CHARLIE resumed a restless pacing about his cabin, angry at his indecisiveness. The puzzle of his three visions nagged at his reason. He stopped before a bookshelf and found what he sought, a copy of Kahlil Gibran's *The Prophet*. Yes, there was a chapter on "Joy and Sorrow." He read it quickly, and more thoughtfully a second time. Two phrases glued to his tired mind:

"Your joy is your sorrow unmasked—they are inseparable."

"The deeper sorrow carves into your being, the more joy you can contain."

He smiled. *So*, he thought, *Doreen was right...joy follows sorrow*. And then he frowned. *But I still can't decide about tomorrow, let alone unravel any mysteries of the future*. He shrugged his shoulders. *My future is for the Gods to decide; who am I to attempt to see what they foretell?*

When he finally went to bed, he was no closer to a decision than when his evening began. Conflicting feelings warred about in his mind. He acknowledged he needed money, but he didn't like pandering to someone else's greed and ambition. He concluded the risks were acceptable, no greater than his burning missions, but he worried about betrayal. Was guiding Alden into the plantations another betrayal? Of Doreen? Of self? And for what? The money? Again the spirit-cursed money.

Threatening his sleep, pain darted back and forth between his shoulders. He threw back his covers and stalked angrily to the bathroom. He'd forgotten his pills. Since diagnosed with arthritis a year before, he'd reluctantly conceded to a pill regimen—when he remembered to take them. Aspirin was okay—but gold pills? The idea of taking gold, even in pill form, was bizarre. *Here I am ingesting natural salts of the Klamath which I have to buy at a drugstore, when nearly every day I float over a lifetime supply for ten thousand sufferers*. He'd rejected other medications recommended. A two-page list of hazardous side effects bothered him more than his pain. *Arthritis, the curse of the river spirits. I wonder what my ancestors did. Probably nothing. If they suffered in silence, I can too.*

His sleep was fitful and dream-interrupted. In his last dream, he was a boy again and followed a man high into the Siskiyou Mountains far from any trail. The man was not his father, but he couldn't see the man's face. Crossing a ridge, they saw below them the lost river of gold gleaming in sunlight. Their descent into the river valley was long, steep, and exhausting. They found the riverside densely overgrown with marijuana plants twenty feet high and guarded by a legion of armed men. Detouring around the guards, they finally reached the river, which contained no gold; but in its swiftest currents swam six pair of giant fish, big and strong enough for a boy to ride. A legless man sat on the bank and held reins which harnessed the fish. He taunted Charlie and refused to relinquish the reins. Across the river, a young woman stared from another marijuana grove. Her face contorted with pain and suffering but then transformed into a smile when she saw Charlie—and he recognized Carleen. He could not look at her, and he dropped his gaze to the river surface, where he saw a mirrored reflection of his companion. The face was Alden's, unmasked and leering with treachery and deceit. As he ran from the river in terror, Charlie awoke in a sweat, his heart racing. He puzzled over the riddle of his dream, but its meaning eluded him.

Then he finally slept the dreamless sleep of exhaustion.

TAWANEESKA
Where the River Weeps

*C*HARLIE ROSE AT DAWN, his dream but fragments of recollection. He felt unrested, irritable, and perplexed. An answer to his dilemma still eluded him. And something else was missing, an unusual absence his sleep-dulled faculties couldn't identify. Then he realized—no truck noises assaulted the morning stillness. He wondered why.

Wincing in anticipation of pain, he began to stretch, and then laughed out loud at another unexpected absence. No pain greeted him. *Drugs still work...sometimes.* Fatigue and irritation disappeared. He walked to the window, opened it, and confirmed the absence of noxious morning sounds. Too gentle to hear, a persistent drizzle drained off the roof and became audible dribbles that fell from the eaves and spattered the ground. He watched vapor mists rise from the Klamath and merge with coarse gray clouds crowding into the valley and obscuring its hillsides. A familiar portrait of autumn, greedy clouds appeared to suck their moisture from the river below rather than the air above, pilfering the river's water in order to quench a thirsty earth. He laughed out loud again. Yes, he lived in a crazy world turned upside down, a contrary world where rivers rained up and raindrops no longer showered down from the sky.

Good, he thought. *We need the season's first important storm, a settling-in rain to raise the river.* He knew the deception in a storm that began politely, windless, and without fury. Soon it would gather intensity, until howling winds shrieked up and down the Klamath gorge. Then, drenching rain would linger for days and end only when mild weather fronting another system eventually pushed it out. He welcomed the storm's ironic promise—bad news for river boats but good news for fish. Nature's renewal message would trigger an upstream migration urge for steelhead waiting at the Klamath's estuary for their first big taste of autumn.

Still angry at his indecisiveness, he fumed at his vacillation over clothing selection. *I can't even decide what to wear.* In frustration, he finally dressed in his fish clothes and laid out a heavy wool sweater and his best Gore-Tex rain jacket with matching rain pants.

He treated himself to a leisurely breakfast: half a grapefruit, a huge bowl of oatmeal with dried cranberries providing an energy boost, three eggs scrambled with fresh spinach, a sausage patty, and heavily buttered toast lathered with Doreen's homemade apple jelly. He brewed fresh coffee, savored the smell and taste of one cup and poured the rest, hot and steaming, into an old metal thermos. After donning the sweater and rain jacket, he retrieved a day-pack from the closet, stuffed in his rain pants, a water-proof match container, and a cook pot with two pairs of heavy ragg wool socks wrapped into the interior. From the kitchen he added two tins of sardines, a box of crackers, a quarter-round of cheese, two packets of powdered soup mix, and six chocolate bars. *I'll save room for lunches from Tony Fisheyes, but I better have extra food just in case.*

Grumbling to himself, he left his cabin and stepped out into morning bleakness. He paused for a moment on the doorstep, and his gaze sought to penetrate the foggy gloom before him. *I need a sign now, some sign from the Hupoks' mountain spirits.* A heavy cloud curtain denied passage to whatever message lay beyond, and he smiled cynically. *No more reliable than the white man's Gods...never there when I need them.*

IN his room, Alden dressed without indecision. He'd slept well and awakened refreshed—and exhilarated by the anticipation of danger. The stormy weather meant little to him, just another logistic to manage. He was prepared. He had added rain gear and a well-used pair of heavy, lug-soled hiking boots to his outdoor garb. A shiny 38-caliber revolver nestled snugly in the shoulder holster concealed below his left armpit. He felt confident Charlie would accept his proposal.

CHARLIE'S van traveled Highway 96 alone. Puddles of rainwater in the oncoming lane, the downriver lane, were clear and undisturbed except for dimpling rings from raindrops. Still no logging trucks. He puzzled about it. Had the logging suspension Straw Hat Harry expected begun already? He wished he'd lingered at Tony Fisheyes last night or paid more attention to the subdued conversations of the few loggers who came in while he dined.

As he approached a narrow bridge spanning Indian Creek, he slowed down. On impulse, he stopped on the bridge and gazed upstream. Far up the valley the clouds parted. For a moment, five peaks and a high western ridge defied enshroudment. Source of the stream of his boyhood basked in rays from a rising sun. Spotlighted and appearing magnified was a stand of virgin spruce and fir trees on the southern flank of Preston Peak. Then the clouds closed and obscured the scene. But his brief view of an unspoiled forest remained imprinted in his mind. His mountain spirits had given him the sign he sought. He finally knew his decision.

BY the time he picked up lunches and reached the River's Edge, his mood had lifted. He remembered something Doreen had told him, "Decide things in the morning, Charlie. Not at night. Your brain's too tired at night." He waited patiently for Alden. To avoid any possibility of being overheard, they would talk inside the van.

"YOU'VE decided?" Alden asked as he climbed into the van beside Charlie.

The man doesn't waste time on small talk, Charlie thought. "Yes, I've decided."

"Well?" Alden was impatient, and Charlie's face didn't betray his decision.

"I won't take you." Charlie was deliberately brief.

Alden's face showed no reaction. "May I ask why?"

"Sure."

"Is it the money? You want more?"

"No," Charlie laughed. "It's not the money."

"The danger then? It's too risky?"

"No. It's not that. I never feel threatened in the mountains."

"Why, then?"

"It's simple enough. I'm through exploiting the Klamath. I won't be a part of anything that exploits the river, its mountains or its forests. This is my home, my world, my life. My dreams were born here, and they'll either be realized or die here. I've seen the Klamath exploited enough, and I've helped do it. But I won't do it anymore. Not for money. Not for anything." Charlie paused, and his eyes bored into Alden. "You're no different from the rest. You're just a different kind of pillager. You're here to exploit the Klamath for personal gain. You'll write a big inside story about our pot growers, collect a nice fee for the scoop, and then move on to your next dramatic revelation. You don't give a damn about what goes on here, or at the growers' camps, and how they affect our lives. To you, it's just another story. There are many stories here…about what's happening to our loggers and other people of the Klamath and their families, what's happening to our forests and their wild creatures, and what's happening to our rivers and the fish who swim there. But you won't write those. They're not sensational, not marketable, particularly for a big fee. No, Mr. Morse, take your money and find someone else. I'll not go back into the mountains for you, not at any price."

Alden squirmed in his seat, but his face was determined. "I thought that might be your answer. And you're right. I'm here to exploit. But not in the way you think." Alden removed a small wallet from a belt strapped around his waist inside his shirt, extracted a card and passed it to Charlie. "Here, you need to look at this."

Charlie studied the laminated identification card. Alden's photograph glared at him. Charlie's head jerked back. "Drug Enforcement Administration? DEA? You're a Fed? A Federal agent?"

"Yeah. And a damn good one."

"Why all the crap about being a feature writer?"

"I needed a cover. I knew my lack of skill might betray a fisherman's guise. A writer is credible cover, and it would have protected both of us. Now that you know who I really am, we're both at great risk." Alden paused and looked intently at Charlie. "Will you help us?"

"I don't know." Charlie's mind swam with conflicting thoughts. Uncertainty gripped him again. "I have to think."

"While you're thinking, let me give you some more information. I've worked this case for nearly a year now...since the DEA transferred me to San Francisco from Mexico City. We're planning one big, sweeping raid next spring...on all the large marijuana plantations in the Klamath National Forest. We want to hit them hard and send a message to other pot farms in other national forests. Our plan is secret. Even local enforcement officials don't know. Before we strike, we need more detailed information, information you can help us with...about the precise locations of plantation sites, how best to approach them undetected, who their leaders are, where to find them, and how they distribute their crops. We want to cripple the entire northern California marijuana system in one raid.

"From aerial surveys and other sources, we already know a lot about what goes on up here. Let me tell you about it...some you may already know. Several years ago the big growers came here seeking hot summers, water, and anonymity. There's plenty of summer heat and plenty of water. Also, few places in the United States outside Alaska provide as much isolation and security as the Klamath region. Over a widespread area, it offers a natural protective canopy...from all the new growth in thousands of forest sections logged thirty to fifty years ago.

"We figure there are more than fifty-thousand acres under

cultivation in the national forests of northern California and southern Oregon. That's maybe half a million high grade sinsemilla plants, about half of it the hand-manicured, top-quality Maui Wowie variety. That's why the growers need imported labor. Their annual crop yield is over 250 tons with a value of one billion dollars. If we can bust a big enough piece of this in one raid and break the marketing network, we'll cripple the syndicates and destroy production and distribution from the biggest concentration of marijuana fields in the United States."

Charlie's mind raced. After all the deception, could Alden now be believed? Trusted? Charlie wanted to trust this man. By the river spirits, he wanted to. "And you want me only to guide you into the plantations?"

"Not just that. If you'll help us, we need you to do the map briefings of all my agents before we strike and to help plan our strike teams, their timing, their complement of personnel, and how they'll be best deployed when we reach the plantations. Will you help us?" Alden repeated his appeal.

"Why should I?"

"I think you know the answer to that. I know it's not the money, although we're willing to pay you a lot more than I've already promised...if you help us finish this mission. I think you're an angry man. I sensed it yesterday. And I think I know why. It's your daughter and her marijuana-related death. I think you want the growers destroyed as badly as we do."

Charlie's eyes blazed with anger. "You bastard. You'd take advantage of my private grief, my private thoughts, like that?"

"Sure. I'm exploiting you. But you can't wage a private war on the growers. Help us do it." Alden thought he could see the answer he sought in Charlie's eyes.

Charlie was silent a moment, then turned in the seat to face Alden. The Hawk's visage only slightly softened. "You're right about my feelings for Carleen. But there's more to it. A lot more. I'll tell you all of it, and you will listen." Then he hesitated. *Why should I explain? Not with anyone, not even with Doreen, have I discussed this.* Once again his Hupok reticence fought with his

Anglo Saxon teaching instincts. Once again his duality tormented him, each heritage seeking control of his mind and his actions. *Yes,* he decided, *someone needs to understand.* Then he continued. "When my daughter died, I journeyed upriver alone in search of an Indian sacred place. It's a secluded, holy shrine for rest and meditation, where soothing waters comfort those who come in mourning. The Hupoks called it Tawaneeska, where the river weeps. Here, the Klamath assumes the anguish of all who mourn and all who are mourned. The river adopts their sorrow for its own and grieves for all who suffer torments of loss and death.

"From the nearest river access, Tawaneeska is a day down-river, deep into a gorge above the Seiad Valley. There, where the river makes a long horseshoe bend, a small waterfall that flows constant throughout the year spills three hundred feet into a raging Klamath cataract.

"When I arrived there, I removed my moccasins, and bare-footed I climbed the cliff beside the waterfall, using ancient and worn notches cut by my ancestors. On the soles of my feet, I felt the touch of all those who sought solace before. Only once I stopped...at a tiny ledge halfway up. There, a sheltered rock face still displays ancient, carved portraits of three Indian Gods: Tora, God of the mountain; Gura, God of the forest; and Wara, God of the river. Beside the Gods are carvings of the creatures who serve as living eyes for the Gods: toraiko, the cougar; guraiko, the bear; and waraiko, the steelhead. Above them smiles a carving of Mora, the sun God, and beside it glares moraiko, the eagle who sees for the sun God. Below them hulks Omah, a giant, manlike creature created by the Gods, the one white men call Bigfoot.

"But the carvings are defaced. All of them. Those who used the river without respect slashed the carvings...again and again. Then they added obscenities and also inscribed their initials...so the identities of those who desecrate are preserved in infamy.

"When I reached the top of the waterfall, my body burned with anger and I perspired freely from exertion. The stream that feeds the waterfall has no name. If it were named, it would be called Emerald Creek. A half-mile above, the stream flows slowly over flat rocks, where sunlight warms its water. Then it drops into a succession of seven deep, calm pools where the warmed water nourishes unusual orchids, cresses, and lilies, and unique varieties of stonewort and quillwort not seen elsewhere on the Klamath. This extensive aquatic vegetation refracts light and fills the pools with a lustrous, gemlike color of deepest green.

"I stopped to rest and bathe in the soothing waters of the first pool. When I looked about me, I saw no trees, only stumps. Of the small forest that once thrived along the stream, only stumps remain. But those ghostly remains testify the forest was remarkable for the variety and size of its trees. Conifer and deciduous trees once grew there side by side…red and silver firs by white and goldencup oaks by sugar and foxtail pines…golden chinquapins and bay laurels by Engelmann and weeping spruces by madrones by Port Orford cedars. And many more I couldn't identify. All were specimens of unusual girths…as if the Gods there preserved only their finest. But all were cut down long ago to provide fuel and cabin timber first for gold seekers and then for fur trappers.

"When I dove down and peered into the depths of the pool, I saw no trout. Fish no longer swim there. When my grandfather was a boy, schools of small trout lived in each pool. The trout were green-backed and gray-spotted, with colors of the rainbow woven into delicate diamond patterns along their sides. Separated from the river and denied access to the sea for centuries by the waterfall, the trout were a pure native strain. Sunlight gilded the trout, and their bodies shimmered with a tawny, yellow hue which, for the male cockfish, turned to flaming crimson in spring. But gold seekers and fur trappers killed all the trout for food, and now the golden trout of the Klamath no longer swim anywhere in the river's system. Now only big orange crayfish and giant salamanders, food the white man disdained, remain in Emerald Creek.

"From the waterfall, it's only a mile to Tawaneeska. When I arrived it was nearly dark, but, still refreshed from my swim, I felt no fatigue. Emerald Creek begins at the cliffs of Tawaneeska, where hundreds of tiny springs bubble from the cliffsides, like giant tears flowing from the eyes of a great rock face. It's here the river weeps…with tears from the hearts of all who mourn and from the souls of all who died. Tears from Emerald Creek purify the Klamath below and cleanse the spirit of all who travel upon it.

"Because it's so remote, few visit Tawaneeska. Most Indians have forgotten it exists. Purity of Klamath Indian bloodlines diminishes with each generation, and few are left who know the stories of the ancients. Those who remember are shamed by the white man's desecrations. When I looked about me, I saw his scattered relics. A few timbers from an old cabin remain by the first spring pool, and a rusted stove pipe rests half in, half out of the sacred water. Beside the timbers are rusted traps and a pile of river marten bones. Long ago the pool water was diverted, and a deep gash in the sandy earth leads to the remnants of a sluice littered with broken shovels, empty tin cans, and other trash from a hundred thoughtless picnickers. Where crystal waters from the pool's outlet gurgled at my feet, I saw a dozen recently emptied beer cans lodged between the rocks.

"Then I looked up. I saw two eagles soaring above the cliffs. They dove until I saw their yellow eyes, and then they screamed at me. They thought me another intruder. I screamed back at them, 'Yes, moraiko, guard well this sacred place. But don't fear me. I come in harmony to replenish Tawaneeska with my tears.'

"All night I sat upon a rock. I closed my eyes and my mind rested…but I didn't sleep. I wept for Carleen, and my tears joined with those of my ancestors. At dawn I rose. Beside me a lone green-tailed towhee bathed in the shallow basin of a streamside rock, using captured water splashed there as Emerald Creek rippled from its outlet. The bird ruffled his neck feathers, dipped his body into the tiny basin of refreshing water, and used his wings to splatter his upper body. The feathers of his rufous cap stood straight up, like the hair of a fresh-washed, crew-cut youth. Unafraid of my presence, he cocked his head, looked at me, and greeted me with his song…mewing catlike notes, first a piercing 'weet—churr', then a burry 'cheeeeee—churr'. I didn't see his mate, and I wondered what had happened to her.

"Just below me in tear-dampened soil I saw a single evening primrose. Its delicate alabaster petals spread wide and glistened with beads of morning dew. Nourished by my grief, the flower had come to full bloom at night. Tears shed for a vanished life created a new life. My grief was gone. But anger remained, an anger Tawaneeska inflamed and could not restrain.

"Now I can tell you why I will help you."

Charlie paused but Alden remained silent, respecting Charlie's request that he listen. Absorbed in Charlie's description of Tawaneeska, Alden was moved by his guide's visibly strong emotion. Charlie drank from his thermos and then resumed. "I want the growers out of our mountains. They are the last to abuse our tribal lands. The rest are gone or on their way out. Gold seekers, fur trappers, commercial hunters and fishermen all exhausted the Klamath's bounty. Now they are gone. Loggers overharvest our forests and litter our landscape with their slash. Soon they will be gone. The growers are last, and they must go. The run-off from their fields poisons our mountain headwaters. The harvest of their fields poisons our minds. Their legacy of hate and fear poisons our souls.

"The growers must leave so the spirits of all my Hupok ancestors can be freed from the last and most profane desecration of their lands. The growers must leave so once again I can walk in the mountains with pride before I die. And the growers must leave so those who come after me can look one day to our mountains and forests and say, 'There are the lands of the Hupoks. The Hupoks are all gone. Like so many living things, they've disappeared from earth. But...look...their lands remain...undefiled. And the river born of those lands and nourished by tears from all the Klamath Indian tribes still flows pure and clean to the sea.'

"Yes, Mr. Morse. You have the answer you want, and you know my reasons. I will help you." Charlie slumped in his seat, drained by the intensity of his feelings and the strain of expressing them to another.

Alden had waited patiently through Charlie's explanations. He had the answer he sought and sighed with relief. Still moved, he placed a hand on Charlie's shoulder and said, "Thank you, Hawk." Instinct told him a handshake offer would not be an appropriate gesture for the situation. No longer the sympathetic listener and now the determined enforcement officer, he asked, "Can we begin the reconnaissance today?"

"Yes. As I was undecided when I left this morning, I packed for a reconnaissance. The rain will help us."

"How long will it take?"

"One week to see the plantations I already know. Longer if we try to see others you've identified from your aerials. I know all the roads and trails."

"Our mission must be secret. No one must know."

"I've thought about that. As I did today, each morning I'll pick up lunches at Tony Fisheyes and meet you here. We'll conceal *Charlie's Pride* in the shed beside my cabin and leave the van and boat trailer at a riverside takeout. We'll use your car to travel old logging roads into the national forest...mine is too easily recognized. Most will readily accept that you have extended your fishing trip and we're fishing on the river."

"Wouldn't it be simpler for you to take time off...a week now and a week in the spring, maybe a few days in between...and let it be known you're with your wife in Eureka?"

"No. Everyone knows I never leave the river for a week. And I'd have to tell Doreen. It's better she doesn't know. Actually, she doesn't want to know...not yet."

Alden laughed. "For a man who first decided to reject my offer, you've thought of everything. You're a good planner, Hawk. We could use you in the DEA on a more permanent basis."

Charlie shook his head and smiled. "No thanks. I'm not impressed with your life expectancy. When the reconnaissance is over, I'll do your briefings and help plan for your strike teams. And, I'll also enlist Straw Hat Harry. He knows the growers' distribution system, and you can trust him. When the raid is over, I'll come back to the river. The fish become too spoiled and complacent when I'm not here bothering them."

"Do you want a gun? I have an extra at the motel."

Charlie again shook his head. "No. I don't do guns...never did. I'm confident I can show you what you need to see without needing that kind of protection."

"One last thing, Hawk. I know you don't like me, but we'll have to trust each other."

"No, Alden. You'll have to trust me. I'm still not sure I can trust you. I'll be watching you carefully. Remember, we travel the high country I've known for fifty years. It will be easy for us to become separated. You'll become lost, and only I will return."

Alden shuddered as he left Charlie's van and stepped out into the rain.

TAWAHUNA
Where the River Ends

BRINGING NEW LIFE to replace the old, spring came quickly to the Klamath. In a natural paradox, renewal began at river's end—the Klamath estuary. Seasonal transformation progressed rapidly against the river's spring snowmelt, like a powerful counter-current that gained strength as it moved higher into the mountains. Far upriver, the results of Charlie's contribution to a different kind of spring transformation were substantial and well publicized. News of successful Easter week raids by the DEA on northern California's marijuana plantations dominated headlines in the San Francisco papers and occupied the entire first page of the Eureka *Times-Standard*. Doreen couldn't wait for Charlie's weekly Saturday-morning call, so she called him on Friday, flushed with excitement. "It's true, Charlie? They destroyed everything?"

He was excited too. "Yes, it's true. The newspapers even got it right. Federal agents busted all the major plantations. They destroyed drying sheds, other buildings, unshipped stockpiles, and all the immature crops. They also captured most of the growers. Some of the small pot farms weren't targeted, so they escaped the raid, but the entire distribution system is broken. The syndicates distribute most of their finished marijuana using private planes flying out of a landing strip at Yreka. The DEA confiscated all the planes and their cargos and arrested most of the syndicate bosses in San Francisco."

"So it's over? The growers are really gone?"

"They're gone, Doreen. All gone. The few growers who weren't targeted fled."

"So, your private war is over too? No more burnings?"

"No more. The Hawk no longer hunts by night."

"Did you see who the agent in charge was? Alden Morse. All the papers interviewed him. Isn't that the fisherman you guided last fall? The feature writer whose offer you rejected?"

Charlie hesitated before answering. "Yes. He posed as a writer."

Suspicion nagged her. "You never really told me...I just assumed." Suspicion became realization and she shuddered. "Charlie, you didn't turn him down. He had to have inside information to plan a successful raid. He got it. And you're the only one who could help him get it. You guided him didn't you?"

"Yes, ultimately I agreed to help him. I just returned from his debriefing last night. I respected your request, and his, not to tell you of my involvement until it was over. I rejected Alden the writer, but I accepted Alden the agent, even though I didn't like him. I still don't. But the DEA does its homework. He analyzed me too well. He knew I wouldn't refuse once he took a big chance and told me who he really was. When the newspapers broke the story, I expected you'd call. I knew you'd figure it out once the reporters got to Alden."

"Oh-h-h, Charlie, does anyone know you were involved?"

"Only the agents and Straw Hat Harry. He helped them destroy the growers' distribution syndicate."

"Did anyone see you when you guided Alden into the plantations last fall?"

"Only at a distance. Except once when Alden's car broke down and a supply truck helped us. The driver knew me. I think he was suspicious."

"So you're still at risk?"

"I don't think so. It's possible, but I'm not going to worry about it."

"Will the DEA agents protect you?"

"No. There's not much they can do. They've all pledged not

to disclose that Straw Hat Harry and I helped them. That's about all they can do. Don't worry. I feel safe here."

"Yes, Charlie the Hawk. On the river, you'll be safe. And proud. Once again you can be proud. What you've done fills me with pride too. Can you tell Michele? She would want to know. She should know. She'll be less angry at you for what happened to Carleen."

"Yes. But not yet. I don't want her to worry about the boys' visit in June."

"What will you do now, Charlie?"

He chuckled. "Get out of here for a while. Avoid the journalists. They've descended on the river like a plague of locusts, but I'm sure their infestation is temporary. There were more newspaper reporters here today than Federal agents in the raid. All the television networks are setting up for local stories this weekend. They've talked to everyone in sight. They were even in Tony Fisheyes last night, interviewing Tommy Two Stumps, the font of Klamath gossip. I'm leaving before they start talking to Indian fishing guides. By the time I return, they'll be long gone to manufacture national interest in some other incident, with emphasis on dramatic rather than insightful coverage."

"Where will you go?"

"First into the mountains, where I want to walk with pride again. I'll try to find the virgin forests at the headwaters of Indian Creek and look for what remains of the Paladora. I plan to climb to the highest point in the Siskiyous…to Preston Peak. I want to be there at sunrise, so I can look down on all the Klamath lands and waters bathed in first light and reflecting first promise of a fresh beginning. I'll stand there, offer thanks to Tora and Gura, and remember what the Klamath was once and imagine what it can be once again.

"Then, I want to spend a few days alone on the river and confer with Wara about bringing more fish into the Klamath. Even though the water is high, I hope to take *Charlie's Pride* and drift from the Hoopa Valley all the way to the sea. I want to see where the river ends. Tawahuna, the Hupoks called it…where the Klamath finally empties into the Pacific. I'll spend an evening there at the estuary, make my appeal to the river spirits and listen to the calls of the loons, grebes, and other water birds who welcome the river's arrival at its final destination.

"Somewhere near the estuary is the site of Wanakoola, the ancient Indian fishing village. I'll try to find it, see if anything remains. I know that a few redwood forests beside the river are preserved. My forebears played and toiled there among those same giant redwoods when the trees were only saplings. I want to stand on the land and walk among the trees in that ancient forest of my people...so I can feel my heritage around me and hear the wind-driven whispers of the ghosts of my ancestors.

"Then I'll come to Eureka...to pick you up and drive down to San Francisco."

Doreen laughed. "The City? The Hawk wants to go to the City?"

"Sure. As long as I don't have to live there."

She laughed again. "Charlie, what will we do?"

He laughed. "Spend money. Lavishly and foolishly. Spend some of the government's money. First I have to pick up a check from Alden. Then we'll stay for a week at the Mark Hopkins hotel. We'll buy you new dresses, one for each day, with matching shoes and jewelry, a fine new coat and handbag, and...and anything you see that you need."

"Charlie-e-e." Doreen was incredulous and blushing. "You know my needs are simple. I don't need anything new."

"I know. But I also know that sometimes there will be a light in your eyes as we walk through the shops. You won't say anything, but your eyes will give you away. It's then I'll know what we should buy."

"But...but what about you? Save something for yourself."

"I will. If you'll help me find a new blue suit, a pinstripe, I'll wear it every day in San Francisco, and then have it cleaned and put away for you to bury me in. And I'll buy a whole shelf of new books, which I'll save to read when I become too feeble to ride the river and fish for steelhead."

"Charlie-e-e." Doreen was still incredulous. "It sounds so extravagant. Can we afford it?"

"Yes. We can. For one week we can afford it. After San Francisco, I'll return to the Klamath and prepare to take our grandsons into Oregon to see Tawahana, where the river begins. And I'll get ready for the next steelhead season. I have a feeling the river spirits will give us a long season of bountiful spawning runs. For the first time in years I think the Klamath will be full of fish—"

"With a hundred steelhead taken by Charlie the Hawk," Doreen finished for him. She was thrilled to hear him so enthusiastic and full of plans for the future. "And...Charlie?"

"Yes?"

"Our trip to San Francisco sounds nice, so nice. It really does. And it pleases me. It pleases me very much. I'll wait for you. Please come soon."

"Two weeks, Doreen. In two weeks I'll come."

———————

CHARLIE REMOVES HIS HAT and leans forward. He lifts his oars and balances their weight with his arms folded over them, his hands clasped above his elbows. He closes his eyes and rests his head on his forearms. Dripping oars are poised just above the water, instantly ready if needed. Afternoon sunshine warms his back and aching shoulders. He feels sweat soak through his shirt and then the shirt begin to steam dry in the sun. Behind him his bow flag flutters at the tug of a sudden upriver breeze, and he senses a change. The wind smell is different. It carries the breath of the sea—Tawahuna's greeting, he's sure of it. He feels relaxed, almost content. But he also feels fatigue's growing tyranny. His body protests his forced pace, and its pain screams at his mind to issue the command to slow down and rest. He's pushed hard for three days, maybe too hard. He knows he's tired now, very tired, but he wants to reach Wanakoola while fair weather holds.

The bridge carrying Highway 101 over the Klamath retreats

a hundred yards behind him. Two families picnicking below the bridge waved at him as he drifted by, and they still stand on the bank watching him. According to his river map, only one last cataract and a few twisting miles remain before he enters the wide, flat water of the Klamath estuary. He can afford to rest now and drift at the river's speed. Impatience concedes to lethargy, and the concession brings welcome relief—to mind and body. As he rests, his body fatigue spreads until his limbs seem numb and weightless. An insistent languor invades his mind. His thoughts are jumbled and unfocused, and then finally untroubled and vacant. The narcosis of exhaustion pushes aside his reason, and his mind gratefully releases control of his body's actions to his senses.

His hears the dull roar of the Klamath's last cataract not far below him. He remembers that the Hupoks believed each rapids marked a place where lovers died, and he wonders who of his ancestors memorialized the Klamath's final fury.

He feels pride swelling inside him again. It's grown stronger each day since Doreen's call. Not a heart pride this time, nor a mind pride. He struggles to remember those. He knows those are lost prides of his youth. He senses this pride is different: a pride in place...or in time? A more conciliatory, self-accepting pride. A maturing pride? Yes. He acknowledges and welcomes it. Now he can identify it. It's the kind of pride that germinates in yesterday's hardship, grows puissant from fighting today's despair, and finally blossoms to conquer tomorrow's challenge; an enduring pride that knows no worldly master; a pride of the senses that radiates powerfully from the soul, surpasses mortal limitations, and denies human indifference.

He first felt his soul pride ten days before, when he crept around a black-tailed doe and fawn sleeping beneath maidenhair ferns in a grove of western yew trees. The newborn fawn curled between his mother's forelegs. His chest heaved with the rapid heartbeats of the very young. His tiny nose snuggled tight to his dam's muzzle.

His soul pride welled again, when he followed a faint path,

a remnant of the Paladora he believed, to a viridescent tarn at the source of Indian Creek. There, he waded through shallows choked with sedge and smelled the freshly blossomed bladderwort. He watched methane marsh gas displaced by his footsteps burble from the bottom ooze through viridian algae undulating like waves across the tarn's surface. He inhaled the ancient smells of natural riparian birth.

And the same feelings overwhelmed him, when he recovered from the exhaustion of his night climb to the summit of Preston Peak, stood in the soft first light of a new day, watched the sun burst into the sky, and then turned a full 360 degrees to imagine his vision for the Klamath stretching to the horizon in every direction. Then again, when tired and cold from sunset's sudden forfeiture of day to the chill of night, he drifted by the river's first redwood tree, a scarred and hoary old survivor, a sentinel silhouetted against the sky and standing alone, defying harvest.

Now he hears the river's last cataract rage louder and closer. As he did as a boy to enhance his images, he closes his eyes. He listens to the Klamath sing its last song of lost love's final passion. The river beckons and commands him to engage all his senses. His soul pride responds with a surge of fresh energy. He opens his eyes, lifts his head, raises his arms, squares his shoulders, drops his oars into the water, and resumes powerful rhythmic strokes pushing his boat forward. Eagerly he answers the river's call.

———

AT THE END of the second week, the day she expected Charlie, Doreen received a call from Straw Hat Harry. Harry struggled with his message, "He's...he's disappeared, Doreen. Charlie's disappeared. The Hawk is gone."

At first she wasn't concerned. "I'm sure he's still at the mouth of the Klamath, Harry. You know Charlie."

"No, Doreen...I'm sorry...but he's gone. The ranger just called from Klamath Glen. They found *Charlie's Pride* yesterday, washed up on the beach at the Klamath estuary. The boat was badly stove below the water line, and both oars were missing.

They recovered Charlie's hat…it was caught under the gunnels… but nothing else. They're still searching the river, but they think he's drowned. Most of the guides left this morning with their boats to help with the search. I'm so sorry."

Doreen was calm, as if she had subconsciously expected the call and prepared herself for it. "He always said the river forgave him too many mistakes. An accident? Or do you think the growers had something to do with it?"

"I don't know. Should I contact the DEA?"

"No. What can they do?"

"Nothing. Call in the FBI maybe."

"No. Don't. Please don't. What does it matter? If the Hawk is gone, he's gone. No one can bring him back. If he's only lost on the river and wants to be found, the guides will find him. If he is truly gone, I don't want his body found. I couldn't bear to see him in death. I'd rather think of him free, finally at peace and resting in the bosom of the river that captured his heart, broke it, and then mended it again.

"If he's found the river's final sorrow, it's fitting he found it at Tawahuna. Perhaps now he finds the river's final joy. Maybe he finally hears the Gods laughing in their gardens at Wateela. Maybe he finally sees there the Omahs, unicorns, dinosaurs, and giant trout of his boyhood dreams. I hope so. And I'll believe that it is so. I'll pray that his final rest is filled with memories of all the joys he found in life and with sounds and scenes of all the joys he sought but couldn't find in life."

"Will you be all right…there alone?"

"Yes. I'll call Michele."

"Are you sure? Rosie wants to drive down."

"I'll be fine. I'll drive to our Klamath cabin tomorrow. I want to wait there until the search is ended."

After saying goodbye to Harry, Doreen walked listlessly into her bedroom and looked at her old suitcase beside the door. She placed the suitcase on her bed, opened it and woodenly removed the clothing she'd packed there with so much care and anticipation the night before. Then she repacked the suitcase with faded blue jeans, two fresh peasant blouses, a pink cardigan sweater, and a red kerchief for her hair—her river clothes, Charlie called them.

Tomorrow she would get up early and drive first to the ranger station at Klamath Glen to retrieve Charlie's hat. She'd forgotten to ask Harry about the flag from his boat. Perhaps that was salvaged too. She hoped so.

She sat on her bed, postponing the call to Michele and not minding being alone. She felt numb, her senses dulled, her mind sluggish with its growing burden of grief deferred. She frowned, shut her eyes and remained quiet a long time. Knowing the shock of loss wears off slowly, she waited patiently for the pain of loss to fight its way into her shock-deadened senses. Death's reality does not quickly follow into consciousness the news of death. Acceptance of finality is begrudging, reluctant, gradual, but inevitable. Anger precedes acceptance and is pain's artificial catharsis. Grief follows acceptance and is pain's natural healing process. Doreen instinctively knew all this and waited.

Finally, when she felt her anger come, she opened her eyes, and, still tearless, she screamed at the empty room, "Why? Why now? *WHY TAKE HIS LIFE NOW?*"

Her screams drained her anger and her mind cleared.

Then she smiled. Her mood lifted and her features brightened as the words from Charlie's favorite Hupok prayer, and their meaning as an answer to her screams, forced their way into the numbness of her mind. She whispered the simple lines:

> *When my day is over*
> *And my work is done,*
> *Release my spirit from earthly bounds*
> *And set me free.*
> *Free to walk the pathway to the sun*
> *And ride the river to the sea.*

When she rose from the bed, she walked to the telephone, gathered up her husband's two photographs, and spoke to them. "So,

Hawk, your prayer is answered. And now you are free, truly free. I pray you're content, forever content. Rest well, my Tamiko. Rest well with the Gods of your fathers."

Doreen was still smiling when she called Michele. Grief would have to wait until later.

EPILOGUE

*D*OREEN PURPOSELY SAVED her last trip to Charlie's cabin for autumn. Fallen maple leaves clustered around the front door step, and she shuffled through them and on inside. Cooler air and silence greeted her, and the musty smell of unoccupied space enveloped her. She paused in the empty front room, where rows and rows of empty bookcases occupied most of the wall space. *Even his books are gone, and I'm surrounded with nothing but memories.* The naked bookshelves stared impassively at her. Gone also was the inviting ambiance of a cheerful home. Now it just felt oppressive. She shivered, wrapped her sweater more securely around her, and walked to the back bedroom, the room she and Charlie had shared for so many years. Disturbed in their descent by a draft from the opening door, unsettled dust particles danced crazily in sunlight streaming through curtainless south windows. She'd scrubbed the windows clean, inside and out, three months ago. Now she noticed they were soiled again and glazed with a film of grime-capturing water spots.

Outside, remnants of a finch's nest protruded from Charlie's hat swaying gently from the limb of an old maple tree, and she frowned. *I wish they'd found his flag.* She suppressed an impulse to retrieve the hat and then smiled. *Leave it,* she decided. *It's the kind of useful purpose he would have wanted, and it should survive at least one winter. I'll ask the new owner not to remove it.*

Inside, two of the windows bathed the bare and dusty floor in a dozen rectangular pools of light. Light from a third window fo-

cused its beams on Charlie's fly-tying desk. Now she was glad the
desk remained. Originally she'd planned to move it to Eureka,
but the new cabin owner, a fisherman from the City, wanted it—
wanted it badly enough to increase his offer price. He'd pressed
her until she reluctantly agreed to leave it.

One of her husband's earliest cabinetry projects, his old desk
showed the stains and scars of years of daily use. But it was sturdy,
ruggedly handsome, and still serviceable, with its dozens of draw-
ers, compartments, and cubbyholes. When they were young, Michele and Carleen had delighted in finding secret places in the
desk to hide things from each other and to surprise their father.
She recalled an evening when she had watched Charlie search
for an illusive patch of rabbit fur and had discovered two frogs
sharing a compartment with his finest feathers and patches. The
frogs were fresh and lively, and Charlie transferred them to their
daughters' beds, where Michele's and Carleen's peals of laughter
turned to squeals of mock disgust.

It seemed appropriate that something so personal to Charlie stay with their cabin. His desk provided a lingering sense of
permanence, a continuity of presence that provided something
else she needed badly at that moment—an enduring sense of
comfort from a long-lasting emotional hug. She walked over,
smiled as she stood in the sunlight, and ran her hands gently over
the desk's scarred surface, remembering how she liked to watch
him tie flies, how she loved to let her fingertips move over each
piece of his newly-finished woodwork, feel a master's touch in
his craftsmanship. His desk and the memories it preserved dis-
pelled the cabin's sterile emptiness. Gone also was its oppres-
siveness.

It was midday in September. On impulse, she left the cabin
and walked around it, searching for Charlie's path down to the
river. It was still there, an opening in the forest barely visible in
the shadows. *It's been so long...but why not?* She made her way
down to the Klamath with difficulty. New vegetation took advantage of a season without use and threatened to ensnare her
feet. The trail was already faint and heavily overgrown with ferns,

alders, and laurels, except where it provided natural drainage. In another year the forest would reclaim its own.

Warm, moist air surrounded her when she reached the river's edge. A heavy cloud bank loomed far in the west. She frowned in disappointment when she realized the sand bar and deep water of the back eddy were gone and Charlie's sun rock was half submerged. Captured by the unusually high water of spring, the sand had all moved downriver—to replenish or create another beach. *In time everything changes.*

The river flow had changed too, and she noticed even the water noises sounded different—less lyrical. *But, look.* She watched a stray current curl in toward shore and surge gently upstream— just a hint of a new back eddy. A promise that time and the river would rebuild their private beach and restore Tawaskeena? *A cycle of life renewed?* She hoped so. Then she saw their cuddling rock and clapped her hands. Unchanged by time, it still basked in sunshine just above the new water line. More images flooded her mind. She gazed into the sky and made the soft, guttural coughing sounds of a river otter at play. Then she looked back to the river and whispered, "Yes, Tamiko, I remember. I'll always remember."